HOW I SURVIVED MIDDLE SCHOOL

I Thought We Were Friends!

Check out these other books in the
How I Survived Middle School series by Nancy Krulik:

HOW I SURVIVED MIDDLE SCHOOL

I Thought We Were Friends!

By Nancy Krulik

SCHOLASTIC INC.

New York   Toronto   London   Auckland
Sydney   Mexico City   New Delhi   Hong Kong

For Amanda and her friends in the Professional Performing Arts
High School Class of '09. Way to go, everybody!

ISBN: 978-0-545-13272-5

Copyright © 2010 by Nancy Krulik

Published by Scholastic Inc. All rights reserved.
SCHOLASTIC, APPLE PAPERBACKS, and associated logos are trademarks
and/or registered trademarks of Scholastic Inc.

12 11 10 9 8 7 6 5 4 3 2 1   10 11 12 13 14 15/0

Printed in the U.S.A.   40
First printing, February 2010

Is Your Life Spinning Out of Control?

HOMEWORK. Choir practice. Basketball tryouts. Going to the mall. Wow! You sure have a lot of activities to keep track of. So are you keeping it all together, or are you spinning out of control? There's only one way to find out. Take a minute from your busy schedule and try this quiz.

1. **Your essay on the causes of the Revolutionary War is due today. What happens when you arrive in history class?**

   A. You realize you've grabbed your Spanish folder instead of your history folder. You'll have to race back to your locker during lunch to get the paper.

If you hand it in today it probably won't be counted as late.

B. Nothing. You already handed in the paper — three days early!

C. You have your essay stapled and ready to hand in as you walk into the classroom.

2. You've got plans to meet your BFFs at the mall. Which of these describes your arrival?

A. You're there 20 minutes early, as usual.

B. You get there right on time.

C. You make everyone wait 20 minutes, but it wasn't your fault. You had to search your room for your phone, and that really slowed you down.

3. It's the weekend! Yay! What are you doing to celebrate?

A. You spend Saturday evening getting dressed for a big party, but are totally surprised when your aunt arrives with the little cousin you promised to babysit. Obviously you forgot to write the babysitting plan on your calendar — again.

B. You have plans to go to a party Friday night and the movies Saturday night. But you're leaving your days free for homework.

C. You're up late on Sunday night doing all of your homework because you didn't do any over the weekend.

4. Good morning! It's six A.M. How do you feel?

A. A little groggy, but you'll be okay after a shower. It took you a while to fall asleep because you were trying to make a mental list of the things you have to do today.

B. Totally exhausted. Maybe you shouldn't have stayed up and watched that movie on TV last night.

C. You're bright-eyed and refreshed.

5. How would you best describe your closet?

A. Very organized, with shelves for shoes, and everything hung up neatly.

B. Kind of messy, but, hey, you're in middle school!

C. The word *disaster* springs to mind.

6. **It's 3:30 on a Wednesday afternoon. What are you doing?**

   A. Racking your brain trying to remember if you have a French test or a math quiz tomorrow.
   B. Studying your biology notes before basketball practice begins in half an hour.
   C. Hanging out with your friends, but you're planning on writing your English paper tonight.

7. **Where's the shirt you borrowed from your best friend?**

   A. Hanging in your closet until you can bring it to her house this weekend.
   B. Under your bed . . . you think.
   C. In the pile of clothes that needs to go in the laundry.

8. **Like most kids, you've got your list of weekly chores. When do you usually do them?**

   A. I do a few chores each day.
   B. On Sunday afternoon — I can't put them off any more by then.
   C. After my dad has reminded me 100 times.

Now it's time to add up your score:

1. A) 3   B) 1   C) 2
2. A) 1   B) 2   C) 3
3. A) 3   B) 1   C) 2
4. A) 2   B) 3   C) 1
5. A) 1   B) 2   C) 3
6. A) 3   B) 1   C) 2
7. A) 1   B) 3   C) 2
8. A) 1   B) 2   C) 3

What does your score say about you?

8-12 points: Wow! Look up the word *organized* in the dictionary and you'll see your picture right there! You really have it all together, which is great because a sense of responsibility is important. Just remember that it's okay to let loose and be a kid once in a while.

13-19 points: You've found true balance in your life. Basically, you're able to hold it together while keeping up the spontaneity! Good for you!

20-24 points: Whoa! Your life is a tornado, and it's blowing out of control. But it doesn't have to be that way. If you take the time to organize your notebooks, closets, and date planners, you might find that you can achieve so much more.

Chapter
ONE

J

Chloe and I are in the art room. Stop by after your student council meeting.

L

I SMILED as I glanced at the text message that popped up on my cell phone just as our student council meeting was finishing up. Two of my closest friends, Liza and Chloe, had stayed after school, too, to work on an art project. That meant we could hang out a little before the late buses arrived to take us home.

I usually don't check my text messages during school hours. It's against the rules to use a cell phone. (In fact, that's one of the first rules in the official middle school handbook!) But student council meetings take place *after* school, and besides, there were no teachers around. So I figured I could peek to see who had texted me without getting in any trouble. After all, kids never care if other kids are texting. That only annoys adults. Or so I thought.

"Jenny, don't you think you should wait to use your phone until after our meeting?" Addie Wilson exclaimed smugly. "I can't imagine there's anything anyone could text to you that's more important than what we're discussing here. You are so rude!"

I frowned. Addie was calling *me* rude for being on *my* phone? She was on her cell phone all day long – in fact, she was an expert at hiding it from the teachers. Addie was just yelling at me to impress the older kids in student council, and to show how dedicated she was.

If that was Addie's plan (and I was pretty sure it was), it worked. The other class representatives seemed kind of annoyed that I'd been checking my texts during the meeting.

"Addie's right, Jenny," Sandee Wind, the eighth grade class president, said. "We just have one more thing to go over, and then you can answer your text."

Addie smiled triumphantly.

I sighed and nodded. "Sorry," I apologized.

"It's okay," Sandee assured me. "When I was in sixth grade I picked up every text message, too. It's what you do when you haven't had a cell phone for all that long."

Addie grinned even wider. She was obviously feeling very proud of herself. Not only had she managed to embarrass me in front of the whole student council, she'd also gotten Sandee to remind me how much older and more sophisticated an eighth grader was than me. Addie was a sixth grader, too – she was the vice president of the sixth grade, and I was the president. But Sandee had only been condescending toward me, which definitely made Addie feel superior. Not that that was anything new. Addie always felt superior.

Her triumphant mood didn't last long, though. I was sitting next to her, so I could hear the quiet hum of her cell phone as she received her own text message. I knew Addie pretty well, and I was certain she was dying to know who had just texted her. But she couldn't check her phone now. Not after she'd made such a huge deal about me doing it. Although I'll bet Addie thought *her* message was important enough to pick up. The Pops think anything any one of them has to say is incredibly important.

The Pops. That's what my friends and I call Addie and her friends. Pops, as in popular. Addie's group is definitely the popular group at Joyce Kilmer Middle School. I don't mean that they have the most friends out of everyone – even though that would be more of a dictionary definition of popular. The *middle school* definition of popular has no relationship to how many people actually like you. It's more about how many people want to *be* like you. And the truth is, at one time or another, everyone, including me, has wanted to be a member of the Pops.

Every middle school has its own group of Pops. They might be called the Queen Bees, the Alpha Girls, or even the A-listers. But they're all the same. You can spot them anywhere. They're the ones with the newest clothes, the best phones, and the most makeup. Of course, in Addie's case, that makeup was only for school. She wasn't really allowed to wear it, so she put it on in the morning and took it off before she took the bus home.

How do I know so much about Addie Wilson? Well, before she and I started middle school, we were BFFs. Okay, maybe just BFs. That forever thing didn't exactly work out for us. Once Addie found her way into the Pops, she dumped me. Just like that. I'd had no say in the matter.

I have to admit, I'd taken being dumped by Addie pretty hard. After all, ever since I could remember, she and I had been inseparable. No matter where we went in elementary school, we were together. No one would ever have thought of inviting Addie Wilson anywhere without Jenny McAfee. And vice versa. But now, Addie got invited all over the place — to the mall, to the movies, to sleepovers, and even to parties. All without me. Addie's events were all strictly Pops only.

Which doesn't mean I don't do anything or go anywhere. I have my own group of friends, too. They're a whole lot nicer than the Pops. And right now, two of them were waiting for me in the art room. I started fidgeting in my seat. I know that being class president is a big responsibility and an honor. But right now I really wanted this meeting to end. Unfortunately, there was still one more order of business.

"I wanted you all to have advance notice that next Tuesday is the annual Career Day," Sandee said. "As student council representatives, I think it's important that we make sure to have some interesting speakers come to our school. I'm currently working on getting someone from the mayor's office to come and tell everyone about what being in local politics is like."

Kia Samson, the seventh grade class president, laughed. "That's shouldn't be too hard, considering your mom is the mayor's assistant."

Sandee smiled. "I'm trying to convince her to actually have the mayor herself stop by this year."

"That would be cool," John Benson, the eighth grade vice president, said. "I don't know who I can bring. Last year my dad came and bored everyone to death talking about the exciting life of a tax accountant."

We all laughed at that. Tax accounting didn't exactly sound like an exciting job. But neither did being in charge of the technical support department of a law firm, which is what my father did.

"It's a busy time of year, with the art show coming up, too, so be sure to remind people that Career Day is important, and they should really try to enlist people to come and talk about their jobs," Sandee said.

At the mention of the art show, I was reminded again that Chloe and Liza were waiting for me in the art room. I was getting very antsy. I couldn't wait for this meeting to be over. So I was especially happy when Sandee said, "Okay, that's all I have. Does anyone else have any new business to bring up?"

No one raised a hand. It seemed we all wanted the meeting to come to an end.

"Then, that's it," Sandee announced. "The meeting's over."

And with that we all stood up, grabbed our backpacks, and hurried out of the meeting room. Addie practically knocked me over on her way out the door.

"Move, Jenny," she barked at me. "I've got to meet Maya in the parking lot. We have something important to talk about. She texted me during the meeting. Of course *I* was courteous enough not to look at my phone while Sandee was speaking."

I rolled my eyes. I suspected whatever she and Maya were going to discuss wasn't so earth-shattering that she had to literally fly out of the school to hear about it. But I didn't say anything. I knew how she felt. I wanted to join my friends, too. I had a feeling Chloe and Liza were having fun in the art room, and I wanted in on it.

But when I reached the art room, I wasn't so sure I wanted to go inside. I could hear Chloe complaining from outside the door.

"Liza, how long does it take to draw a face?" she demanded.

"It's taking a lot longer to draw yours than most people's," Liza answered. "If you would just sit still . . ."

I had to laugh at that. Asking Chloe not to move was kind of like asking the earth to stop spinning. Chloe could not sit still, ever.

"Hey, guys," I said, smiling cheerfully in an attempt to defuse what I could already sense was a tense situation.

"Hi, Jenny," Chloe said, leaping up from the stool she'd been sitting on. "How was the meeting?"

"Will you sit down?" Liza demanded. "I want this picture to be right. It's part of my exhibit for the art show."

The annoyance in Liza's voice surprised me. Of all of my friends, Liza was the calmest and most patient. She hardly ever got stressed or angry. But Chloe obviously had been making her nuts.

"You've already made five sketches of my face," Chloe told Liza.

"This is the last pose, Chloe, I swear," Liza assured her.

"But we've already been here an hour," Chloe moaned. "How long am I supposed to sit still and help you?"

I knew the answer to that one. *As long as it takes.* Chloe couldn't just get up and leave in the middle of posing for Liza's picture. That would be breaking an important middle school rule. Not the kind of rule you find in the official middle school handbook (which I had read from cover to cover). This was more the kind of rule that's between kids. But that doesn't make it any less important.

MIDDLE SCHOOL RULE #38:

DON'T VOLUNTEER TO HELP OUT A FRIEND WITH A PROJECT OR HOMEWORK ASSIGNMENT UNLESS YOU REALLY INTEND TO HELP. IT'S BETTER TO TURN SOMEONE DOWN RIGHT AWAY THAN TO DISAPPOINT THEM AT THE LAST MINUTE.

"Come on, Chloe," I urged. "Just sit there. The more still you are, the quicker Liza will be finished. Besides, do you know how lucky you are to have Liza doing your portrait?"

Chloe couldn't argue with that. She knew what a great artist Liza was. We all did. That's why my friends and I had volunteered to be part of her project. Liza was doing a portrait of each of her friends. Then she was going to put all the portraits together into one giant mural, which she was calling *You've Got to Have Friends*.

It was going to be amazing. She'd already done a portrait of my friend Josh that showed him surrounded by mathematical formulas. It totally made sense since Josh is a math genius. Even though he's in sixth grade, he's taking seventh grade math and acing it!

Then Liza drew a portrait of my friend Marc holding his video camera. That pretty much said it all, since Marc was never without his camera. He was constantly filming things for the documentary film he's working on about life in a typical middle school.

Liza also drew our friend Sam (short for Samantha), who just moved here from England, and the twins, Marilyn and Carolyn. In the twins' picture she'd drawn them staring at each other. Marilyn and Carolyn look so much alike that it was almost as though each of them was looking in a mirror.

Chloe was the next person on Liza's list. Then she was going to do one of Felicia and Rachel in their basketball uniforms. I was the last person, mostly because with all my student council meetings lately it was hard for us to find a day that we were both free for me to sit for her.

"Okay, that's it," Liza said as she lifted up her pencil and stepped back to get a good look at the drawing. "That's exactly the pose I wanted!"

"You're finished?" I asked.

Liza nodded. "I think it's going to be good."

"Ooh, let me see!" Chloe said as she rushed around to try to get a glimpse of the sketch Liza was removing from the easel.

Liza shook her head. "Not yet. This is just in pencil. I'll let you see the final portrait once I've painted it. I'm going to do that tomorrow in art class."

Chloe frowned, but she knew better than to argue with Liza about this. Liza was very protective of her artwork. She never let anyone see anything she was working on until it was completely finished. And Chloe, like all of Liza's friends, respected her artistic process.

Just then, Ms. Young, the art teacher, opened the door and peeked into the room. "Sorry, Liza, but you have to head home. I have somewhere I need to be, and I've got to lock up the art room before I go."

"We're just finishing up," Liza assured her.

"Good," Ms. Young said. "See you tomorrow in class."

"You bet!" Liza exclaimed. She sounded so happy. Liza loved art class more than anything.

I'm really fascinated by Liza's talent. That's probably because I'm not exactly what anyone would call artistic. I've sort of mastered drawing a flower, but that's taken me all year. And my drawings aren't exactly what you might find hanging in a museum somewhere.

But *everything* Liza draws is a work of art. Even the little doodles that she scribbles all over her backpack and binders are cool. Those sketches of flowers, eyes, dogs, and cats that she draws absent-mindedly are a million times better than anything I've ever seen my other friends work hard to draw in art class.

"We have a few minutes until the bus comes," Chloe said as she, Liza, and I walked down the hall of the B wing and out into the school parking lot.

"Good," I said. "It's pretty nice out. And I definitely need some fresh air before I go home. That student council room was so stuffy."

"Probably because Addie Wilson was filling it with all of her hot air," Chloe joked.

I laughed. As usual, Chloe had said what the rest of us were thinking. Having Addie on the student council with me definitely took some of the fun out of being class president. But not all the fun. I actually liked being part of student government. It meant I got to find out about things ahead of time. And, therefore, so did my friends. Which is why I was just about to tell them about the upcoming Career Day. But before I could open my mouth to speak, Chloe stopped me.

"Whoa! Check that out," she said, pointing to the area of the parking lot where the teachers parked their cars.

"What?" Liza asked.

"Ms. Young. She's getting into Mr. Strapp's car," Chloe told her.

"So?" I asked. I didn't see what the big deal was. Why would Chloe care if the art teacher was getting a ride from the computer teacher?

"So, that means they're going somewhere *together*," Chloe explained.

I shrugged. "I repeat. So?"

"*So* don't you think that's interesting?" Chloe asked Liza and me. "That means Ms. Young rushed us out of the art room so she could meet up with Mr. Strapp. I wonder what they're up to."

Liza shrugged. "They're probably just carpooling to save gas or something."

"Could be," Chloe agreed. "But maybe it's more than that."

"What?" I asked her. "Like a date or something?"

"Exactly," Chloe said. "It's almost dinnertime. Maybe he's taking her out to dinner. Or dancing."

Liza laughed. "You know what, Chloe? Instead of being an actress when you grow up, I think you should be a writer. You make up great stories."

Chloe shrugged. "I'm just saying it's possible," she said with a grin. "And kind of fun to think about."

Chapter
TWO

CHLOE WAS RIGHT. It was fun to think about the possibility that Ms. Young was going out with Mr. Strapp. It was also kind of weird. I mean, what kid likes to think about her teachers doing normal people things like going out on dates? It's almost as weird as thinking about your parents doing stuff like that when they were young.

But that night, as I sat at my desk, I found myself thinking about Mr. Strapp and Ms. Young. It was infinitely more interesting than trying to figure out the answers to the math problems in the textbook I had on my desk in front of me. The problems were really hard. I hate working with fractions. (Actually, to be honest, it didn't matter that this homework was with fractions. It could've been decimals, or word problems, or even geometry. Math just isn't my favorite subject.)

For a minute, I thought about calling Josh and asking him for help with my homework. But then I remembered that he'd been at a math team meet all afternoon. I figured there was only so much math someone — even a whiz like Josh — could handle in one day. So instead, I decided to log on to my computer to see if maybe there were some easy suggestions for how to add, subtract, multiply, and divide fractions.

But after a few minutes of staring at math websites, my head began to spin. I needed a break. So I decided to check out my favorite website: middleschoolsurvival.com. The first thing I saw was a quiz called *Numerology: Your Personality by the Numbers*.

Ugh! I couldn't believe it. Even my favorite website was pushing math on me tonight. I was totally convinced it was a conspiracy!

Still, I'd never had a bad experience trying something that was posted on middleschool survival.com. So, I decided to find out what this numerology thing was all about.

Did you know that your name can determine the kind of person you will turn out to be? At least that's what believers in numerology say. Numerology is an ancient science that can be traced all the way back to the ancient Greeks and Babylonians. The theory behind it is that everyone's personality can be linked to one of nine basic personality types, all based on the letters in your name.

According to numerology, each of the letters in the alphabet corresponds to a number between one and nine. The chart looks like this:

1	2	3	4	5	6	7	8	9
A	B	C	D	E	F	G	H	I
J	K	L	M	N	O	P	Q	R
S	T	U	V	W	X	Y	Z	

To find out your numerology number, write out your whole name (numerology won't work if you leave out your middle name or use a nickname). Then use the chart to add up the numbers in your name.

I did what the website told me to do. I made my own name chart:

J E N N I F E R A N N E M C A F E E
1 5 5 5 9 6 5 9 1 5 5 5 4 3 1 6 5 5

That added up to 85. But 85 wasn't a number between one and nine. Lucky for me, middleschool survival.com had anticipated that problem. The next part of the instructions told me exactly what to do.

Since there are only nine personality types on the chart, you must add up the numbers in your total to make a single digit. For instance, if the letters in your name add up to 86, add the 8 and the 6 to make 14. Then add the 1 and the 4 to give you the number 5.

So I added up the eight and the five to get thirteen. Then I added the one and three to get four.

But what did being a four say about the kind of person I was? Quickly, I scanned the personality chart to see what it said about my personality.

Ones: Ones are natural born leaders. People follow them because they seem to intuitively know where the fun and excitement are. Ones are amazing organizers, and they are the first people to call on when you want someone on your bake sale or school dance committee. However, sometimes ones can have a tough time sharing the work and the spotlight.

Twos: Twos are quiet people. They make great listeners, and often use their words sparingly. These characteristics make them great friends but can also cause them to get lost in the crowd. That's a real shame because twos are the kind of people who should be celebrated for the loyal friends they are.

Threes: Three's a crowd, but that's okay, because a crowd is where a three is most comfortable. Threes have a knack for making everyone around them feel good about themselves – mostly because threes have such positive attitudes. Threes have a definite sense of right and wrong, and will fight for what they believe in. The tough part about being a three is that they are often extremely sensitive to criticism.

Fours: Fours are extremely responsible people. They're really mature, but no one seems to mind that they're the most grownup people in the group. Their outgoing nature makes fours very popular. However, fours tend to speak before they think, and sometimes they can be a little cruel. Still, they're quick to apologize when they hurt someone's feelings.

Fives: Fives are adventurous and spontaneous. They're exciting to be around because they're always on the lookout for the next experience. They don't wait around for things to get boring. When the activity starts to get dull, they move on. The biggest problem for fives is their lack of ability to plan ahead. This can make some of their adventures seem more like disasters.

Sixes: If you're in need, call a six indeed. Sixes are very caring friends. They'll do anything to help, and they rarely ask anything in return. Sixes are also very trusting souls. That can be their downfall, though, because they can sometimes be taken advantage of. Sixes need to practice saying no once in a while.

Sevens: Sevens are the trendsetters of the middle school world. They're always up on the newest musical groups, the latest fashion trends, and the coolest hairstyles. They're also deep thinkers who like philosophical discussions. Sevens tend to be perfectionists who will settle for nothing less than an A on an assignment.

Eights: Eights are very disciplined and they have a great skill when it comes to concentrating on a task. Eights are also very generous and caring, and they can be great friends. But watch out! They can also be strong opponents, and they tend to hold grudges for a long time if they – or their friends – are burned by someone.

Nines: What the world needs now is more nines. They are the ones who take up the cause of cleaning the earth, stopping the wars, and feeding the hungry. That's an amazing characteristic to have, because energetic nines have all the enthusiasm needed to achieve these big goals. Unfortunately, while they are out saving the world, nines have trouble focusing on the problems of their individual pals. It's not that they don't care, it's just that they don't realize how much the people around them need them, too.

Reading about my number was really interesting — and pretty accurate. I like to think I'm a responsible kind of kid. It would be impossible to be sixth grade class president if I wasn't. That job requires a *lot* of responsibility. And I'm outgoing, too. Maybe not as outgoing as Chloe, but then again, who is?

However, that part about fours being cruel really stung me. I try hard to be nice whenever I can. Still, I have said some pretty nasty things from time to time. But I only said them to the Pops, and they're pretty cruel themselves. So I wasn't one hundred percent sure that it counted.

I glanced back one more time at the characteristics for my number. *Hmmm.* As a responsible four, there was only one thing to do. I had to get back to doing my math homework. Maybe with a little more concentration, and a whole lot of luck, I might get through those fraction problems after all.

Sometimes a girl can totally score by being a four. A person whose name had come up with another numerology number might have given up on that math homework, but not a trusty four like me. I always do all of my homework. I'd answered every question, and, according to my math teacher, I'd managed to get most of them right after all. And I'd done it all by myself.

So I was feeling pretty good about myself as I walked into fifth period lunch the next day. Chloe was already there, sitting at our regular lunch table, right next to Sam. Josh and the twins were at the table, too. And I could see Marc over in the sandwich line, buying his lunch.

"Where's Liza?" I asked as I placed my food tray on the table and sat down beside Josh.

"In the art room," Sam said. "Where else would she be?"

"She's in there a lot of the time now," Marilyn said.

"*All* of the time," Carolyn corrected her sister. "Ms. Young even gave her a pass to get out of her computer class so that she could go work on her project."

"I'm sure she had plenty of time to talk to Mr. Strapp about excusing Liza from class," Chloe said with a grin. "I mean while they were out for dinner, or on the dance floor, or waiting for the movie, or . . ."

"Whoa, rewind that a bit, would you, chum?" Sam asked in her sophisticated British accent.

"Jenny, Liza, and I saw Ms. Young and Mr.

Strapp going off on a date last night after school," Chloe said. She had a triumphant smile on her face. Clearly she was happy to know some hot gossip before anyone else did.

Except Chloe didn't actually *know* anything. At least not anything concrete. She had no idea what was actually going on between our teachers. None of us did. "We saw them get in a car together after school," I explained to my friends. "Chloe just concocted the whole date thing in her overly dramatic imagination. For all we know, Mr. Strapp was giving Ms. Young a ride home because her car was in the shop."

"You have your opinion and I have mine," Chloe said.

"Exactly," I told her. "Besides, I have some *real* news for everyone."

Chloe frowned. She really hated it when someone stole her thunder. And usually I hated doing that to her. But I had a responsibility as sixth grade president to spread school information, and I was determined to do my job.

"There's going to be a Career Day here at school," I told my friends. "It's going to be a huge fair that's held in the gym. There will be tables set up with people from different companies seated at them. We all get to spend time walking around to the different tables, learning about what kind of jobs people do. Because I'm on the student council, I'm supposed to ask people if they can get their parents or their parents' friends to come and talk about different professions. I know it's going to be hard finding people with interesting jobs. I mean, my mom doesn't work, and my dad just plays around with computers all day, but if you guys know anyone . . ."

"I bet our parents would come and talk about the bakery they own," Marilyn told me.

"And they can bring those minicupcakes," Carolyn added.

"Everyone loved those last year," they agreed at the same time.

Sam laughed. "There goes that twin thing again." She smiled at me. "I can ask my dad to pop over and talk to some kids about his job," she said.

"Where does he work?" I asked her. I had no idea what Sam's dad did for a living. She was new to our town, and I didn't know her parents that well.

"Right now he works in the advertising department for a British airline," Sam said. "But he used to be a pilot. He's flown all over the world. I think the only continent he hasn't been to is Antarctica."

"Wow!" Chloe exclaimed. "That is *so* cool!"

"My mom does research at a hospital," Josh

added. "She could probably come and discuss how they're trying to find new ways to cure diseases."

"What are we talking about?" Marc asked as he put his tray down next to Chloe's and grabbed a seat.

"Career Day," Marilyn and Carolyn said in unison.

"Jenny's recruiting people to invite their parents," Josh explained.

"Oh," Marc replied. Like the twins and Liza, Marc was a seventh grader, so he'd been to Career Day last year. "I'm sure my dad will come by to talk about what it's like to work for a sporting goods company. Last year he brought a bunch of wristbands to give out. People seemed to like them."

"I didn't know your dad worked for a sporting goods company," I said.

"Yeah," Marc told me. "He figures out which athletes would be the best ones to hire to do commercials for sneakers, or tennis rackets, or skateboards."

"So your dad knows professional athletes?" Sam asked.

Marc shrugged. "Sure. It's no big deal."

"It will be a huge deal to Felicia," Josh said. "You know how into basketball she is."

We all started to grin, which made Josh blush. He knew we all knew that Felicia was his girlfriend.

But it still sort of embarrassed him. "And Rachel, because she's on the basketball team, too, of course," he added hastily.

"Oh, *of course.*" Chloe giggled.

"What about your folks, Chlo?" Sam asked her. "Do you think either one of them can come and speak on Career Day?"

Chloe shrugged. "It's hard for my mom to get time off from her job to do anything. And my dad just started working again. Plus, he's gone back to school at night."

That surprised me. I'd never heard of a grown-up going to school before. "He has?" I asked her.

Chloe nodded. "He wants to learn how to install solar heating tiles on the roofs of houses. He thinks that in the future, jobs that help save energy will be very important. And he doesn't ever want to be out of work again."

I nodded. It had been really hard on Chloe and her parents when her dad had been out of work. Things were better now, but I totally understood if her parents weren't able to take a morning off to come to school for Career Day.

Besides, I wasn't even sure what *I* was going to do about Career Day yet. Compared to other people's parents, I thought my dad's job would sound dull. I was afraid no one would want to talk to him about it, and he'd be sitting there at his little table all by himself. How embarrassing would that be? But my mom was a stay-at-home mom, so there was nothing for her to come and talk about. My grandparents lived pretty far away, so I couldn't ask my grandfather to come and talk about what it was like teaching biology at a college, which is what he did before he retired. That meant the only person I had to volunteer for Career Day was my dad.

I was distracted from my Career Day dilemma by the parade of Pops that began to pass by our lunch table. Not that it was unusual for Addie and her friends to march by our table. The Pops passed us every day on the way to their meeting in their clubhouse. Okay, so it wasn't really a meeting, and they were actually on their way to the bathroom, and not a real clubhouse. But every afternoon during lunch they all went to the girls' room together to put on makeup and gossip. So that's what I called it.

"Here comes the loo crew," Sam said, making a point of looking at her tray and not at the oncoming Pops.

A moment later, Addie, Dana, Sabrina, Maya, and Claire came parading right past us. As always, they stopped near our table to make some snide remark. Today, their chosen victim happened to be Chloe.

"Oh, nice T-shirt, Chloe," Sabrina said. "But didn't anyone tell you it's cold outside today?"

"They don't make sweaters with stupid sayings on them," Dana told Sabrina. "And if it doesn't have words on it, Chloe won't wear it."

That was actually the truth. Chloe loved T-shirts with clever sayings on them. Today her shirt had a picture of a fish on it. The fish was about to eat a worm that was attached to a fishing line. Underneath the picture it said, *Going Online?*

"I actually think that shirt is very cool," I told Dana. I was determined to stand up for my friend.

Sabrina, Maya, Dana, and Claire all laughed. Addie, on the other hand, smiled pleasantly. "I agree," she told me.

Everyone – my friends *and* the Pops – stared at her. Had Addie Wilson just agreed with me? Had she actually said something nice about Chloe's shirt?

"What?" Addie asked all of us. "It *is* cool." She paused for a minute. "Of course, you all know what cool stands for, don't you?"

"What?" Claire asked her.

"Constipated, Overrated, Out-of-style Loser," Addie said.

I rolled my eyes. I should have known. When was I going to learn that Addie Wilson no longer had a nice bone in her body?

The Pops all began to laugh. "Good one, Addie," Dana said, giving her a high five.

"Thanks," Addie said. She grinned and walked off triumphantly. The other Pops followed close behind her.

"See ya later, suckers," Sabrina said.

As soon as they were gone, I looked over at Chloe, hoping she wasn't too upset by what had just happened. I knew if Addie had just said something that mean to me – which she'd done, many times – I'd be mortified.

But Chloe was laughing. And not the fake, pretending-it-doesn't-bother-me-at-all kind of laughter, either. This was the real deal.

"That was actually pretty good," Chloe said. "Constipated, overrated, out-of-style loser. I'll have to remember that one."

I smiled over at Chloe. "You're amazing," I told her.

Chloe smiled back. "I know," she assured me. "We all are. That's why I never take anything the Pops say seriously. What do they know?"

The Pops might not have known a whole lot, but they sure did keep talking. Addie and Dana didn't shut up once the whole next period during gym class. I know gym is the one time during the day (other than lunch) when you can talk to your friends, but Addie and Dana were totally taking it to the extreme.

"So do you have any ideas about who you can ask to come to Career Day?" Addie asked Dana while they did their jumping jacks. Well, I should say while *the rest of the class* was doing jumping jacks. Addie and Dana were just kind of standing there in the back, waving their arms around.

"You know my mom used to work at Channel Three before she had my sister and me, right?" Dana replied. "Well, she still knows a bunch of people over there. I'll get her to ask one of the newscasters to come and talk about being a TV reporter."

"That's perfect!" Addie exclaimed. "My dad's job is kind of boring."

I smiled. It was nice to know that Addie was in the same boat as I was.

"But my *mom's* a nurse, and that's kind of cool," Addie continued.

I frowned. I'd forgotten about Addie's mom. She was right — being a nurse was a cool job. (And not in that constipated, overrated kind of way. It was *really* cool.) Once, back when Addie and I were still BFFs, Addie's mom had taken us both on a tour of the hospital. I'd liked seeing the operating rooms (we only saw an empty one, of course) and visiting the nursery. The newborn babies were so cute. And then there was this huge life-size doll she let us play with. I thought for a moment. What was her name again?

"I'm going to ask her to bring Rescusi Anne," Addie said as she continued talking to Dana.

I smiled. Rescusi Anne. That was the doll's name!

"Who's that?" Dana asked.

"Rescusi Anne is a doll that they use to teach people how to do mouth-to-mouth resuscitation," I answered her. Then I gulped. *Oops.* I'd just totally admitted that I'd been listening.

"Jenny, do you have to eavesdrop on every conversation I have?" Addie demanded angrily.

"No."

Dana laughed. "Just the ones you have when she's around," she told Addie. "She can't hear you when you're not in the same room — even with those huge ears of hers!"

I blushed beet red. I was so red that I could feel the heat bouncing off of my cheeks.

"Addie! Dana!" our gym teacher called out. "Stop moving your mouths and start moving your legs!"

Addie and Dana got very quiet and started really doing their jumping jacks. I was very relieved. Now they were too busy to keep making fun of me. But I knew it couldn't last forever. After all, making fun of other people was the Pops' favorite thing to do!

Chapter
THREE

IT DIDN'T TAKE LONG for Addie to start in on me again. We didn't have any classes together after gym, but we did ride the same bus home. The minute the school bus pulled out of the parking lot at the end of the day, Addie began making fun of me all over again. I was sitting there, all by myself, minding my own business and reading my text messages. Addie was two seats back, in the middle of the bus, where she always sat.

"Oh, wow!" I exclaimed excitedly. "How cool is this?"

"Talking to yourself, Jenny?" Addie said.

Everyone else on the bus started to laugh. Not that I blamed them. I was sitting there, all by myself. Which meant I'd just asked myself a question — out loud.

I started to blush again. "N-no," I stammered nervously.

"You're not talking to yourself?" Addie asked me. "But there's no one near you. Are you talking to an imaginary friend? I don't blame you. Your real-life friends are all weirdos."

The kids on the bus laughed harder. My face turned redder. Now I was embarrassed *and* mad. "My friends are not weird!" I shouted back at Addie. "And I don't have an imaginary friend. I was just excited because I got a text message from my mom."

Now the laughter got even louder. The kids on the bus were in absolute hysterics.

I sighed. I had just made a total geek out of myself in front of a whole busload of kids. What could be dorkier than saying that you were excited about getting a text from your *mother*?

But I *was* excited. My mom hardly ever texted. It took her forever to get the letters right, so she usually preferred calling. But she would never call me during the school day, since she knew my phone would be turned off. By texting me, she knew I would get her message the minute I got on the bus and turned my phone back on. Obviously, it was very important to her that she reach me. Something exciting was happening back at my house, because the text from my mom read:

Big surprise at home. You will be very happy.

I sat back in my seat and kept my mouth shut for the rest of the bus ride. I wasn't going to give Addie Wilson any more ammunition to use against me. My mother had assured me that I was about to be very happy. I wasn't going to let anyone — not even Addie Wilson — ruin that!

As soon as the bus pulled up to my stop, I hurried off and raced the two blocks to my house. Then I burst in the front door.

"I'm home, Mom!" I shouted. "Where's the surprise?"

"We're in the kitchen!" my mother called back.

We're? Was that some sort of clue? "Who's we?" I shouted.

"Come see," my mother said playfully.

I zoomed through the living room straight to the kitchen. And there, sitting in the seat my dad usually sits in, with a big cup of coffee in her hands, was my surprise.

"Aunt Amy!" I exclaimed. Then I ran over and gave her a huge hug, almost spilling her coffee.

"Hi to you, too," my aunt laughed.

"I can't believe you're here!" I squealed joyfully.

"I have a few days off, so I figured I'd come visit my favorite niece."

I laughed. "I'm your *only* niece," I reminded her.

"Even if your mom had a dozen kids, you'd still be my favorite," Aunt Amy assured me.

I smiled. Aunt Amy always knew exactly the right thing to say. She was incredible and really fun to be around. She was one of the most excit-ing people I knew, which is why I was surprised she was visiting. Life around here isn't exactly exciting.

"You had a few days off and you wanted to spend them *here*?" I asked her.

My mother and my aunt both gave me strange looks.

"I mean it's so boring," I explained. "You live in New York. There must be a million fun things to do there while you're on vacation. Like, you could go to the Empire State Building, or Broadway, or the Statue of Liberty, or . . ."

Aunt Amy shook her head. "I'm flying off to China on business a week from Saturday, and I thought I could use a few quiet, restful days here with you guys before I go. Besides, I *live* in New York. I walk past the Empire State Building every day on the way from the subway to my office, and I can see the Statue of Liberty from my apartment window. I'd rather vacation here and hang out with you and your mice."

I grinned. Most adults hated my two pet white mice. Even my mom wasn't exactly crazy about them. But Aunt Amy *liked* mice. In fact, she was always saying that one day she was going to create a whole line of greeting cards with pictures of mice on them.

That's what my aunt does. She's the art director for the Connections Greeting Card Company. She flies all over the world, meeting artists and checking on the factories where the cards are manufactured. That was probably why she was flying to China – a lot of the company's greeting cards are printed overseas. My aunt Amy definitely has a very exciting career.

Career! Suddenly a bright, broad smile flashed across my face. Now I was doubly glad Aunt Amy had arrived. "Are you still going to be in town next Tuesday?" I asked her.

Aunt Amy took a sip of her coffee and nodded. "Mmhmm. My flight's not until a week from Saturday."

"Great!" I exclaimed.

"Why?" Aunt Amy asked me.

"Well, Career Day at my school is on Tuesday, and since I'm on the student council I sort of have to bring someone," I explained. "I was probably going to get stuck asking my dad."

My mother burst out laughing. "I'm sure your father would be thrilled to hear you put it that way," she teased.

I blushed a little. "I didn't mean it that way," I said. "I just meant that Dad's job isn't that fascinating – at least not to kids. He just goes to an office, works on computers, and comes home. It's the same thing every day."

"I suspect it's a little more interesting than that," my mother said. "But I see where you're coming from."

"Aunt Amy, your job is *really* interesting," I said. "And since you're on vacation, you won't have to ask your boss for a day off to do this, the way my dad would have to."

"That's true," Aunt Amy said. "I'm free as a bird."

"Then you'll come?" I asked her.

"Definitely," Aunt Amy said with a grin. "Anything for my Jennifer Juniper."

I smiled at my aunt's nickname for me. "Aunt Amy, can I ask you one more favor?" I said.

"What?"

"Please don't call me that at school."

Aunt Amy chuckled. "No problem, *Jenny*."

The next day I hurried into the school building as soon as I arrived. I raced over to the student council office and wrote my name on the Career Day sign-up sheet that was posted on the door.

Student: Jenny McAfee   **Guest:** Amy Andrews, Art Director, Connections Greeting Cards

Then I slipped my pen back into my book bag and began to walk down the hall toward my locker.

"Hey, Jenny, wait up!"

I stopped and turned around at the sound of Liza's voice. "You're here early," I said. "Half the buses haven't even arrived yet."

"I didn't take the bus," Liza said. "My dad drove me here because I have my portfolio with me." She glanced down at the big leather case she was carrying. "I finished my painting of Chloe last night. I wanted to bring it in and store it with the others I've done."

"That's great," I told Liza. "Your display is going to be the best one at the entire art show."

"I hope so," Liza said. "I've been working hard enough on it. So how come you're here so early? You never come in from the parking lot until the first bell rings."

That was true. I liked hanging out in the parking lot and talking to my friends until the last possible second. "I wanted to get over here and sign up for Career Day. My aunt Amy said she'd come. You'd love her, Liza. She's an art director for a card company." I paused for a minute. Suddenly I had a great idea. "You should meet her. She loves to talk about art. And I bet she'd really like to look at some of your stuff."

"You think she'd do that?" Liza asked me. "It would be so awesome to talk to someone who could tell me what I would have to do to be a professional artist."

"I know she would talk to you," I assured Liza. "But I don't think you should wait for Career Day. There will be too many kids around for you guys to really have a conversation. Are you free after school today?"

Liza thought for a minute. "I guess so. Rachel and Felicia are posing for their picture tomorrow, and I finished Chloe's."

"Great! Then you can come over to meet Aunt Amy," I said.

"Cool," Liza said. She sounded really excited. And that made me really happy. I always love it when I can do something nice for my friends.

A few minutes later, Liza and I reached the art room. But the lights were out, and the door was locked.

"That's weird," Liza said. "Ms. Young is always at school early."

I shrugged. "Maybe she's going to be absent today."

"I hope not," Liza replied. "I hate when we have a substitute teacher for art class. Ms. Young usually lets me work on my own projects no matter what the rest of the class is doing. But substitutes never do that."

I nodded understandingly. I could see how trying to make a collage with tissue paper or creating a clay coil pot would seem dull to someone like Liza. It was really nice that Ms. Young was so willing to let her develop her talents.

I looked down the hall and smiled. Ms. Young was coming toward us . . . with Mr. Strapp. "I'm glad Chloe's not here right now," I said.

Liza laughed. "I know. If she saw them talking to each other again she'd have them planning their wedding already."

"Chloe definitely likes to create drama," I agreed.

"Even when there's nothing there to create," Liza said.

I grinned. But as I looked at how happy Ms. Young seemed right now, I had to wonder if there really *was* nothing there. Was it possible that Chloe could actually be right about something for once?

"Hi, Liza. Hi, Jenny," Ms. Young greeted us.

"Hi, girls," Mr. Strapp said. Then he coughed a little, the way adults sometimes do when they're uncomfortable.

"Hello," Liza and I replied at the same time.

I started to giggle. "We're kind of like the twins," I said. Then it was Liza's turn to laugh.

Ms. Young and Mr. Strapp smiled at us, but I could tell they didn't really get the joke. Why would they? Marilyn and Carolyn didn't have any classes together. And they could only do their "twin thing" when they were in the same place at the same time. So Mr. Strapp and Ms. Young didn't understand.

"I've got to get to the computer lab and set things up for first period," Mr. Strapp said. "I'll talk to you later, Emily."

"Okay. See you later, Chas," Ms. Young answered. She watched as Mr. Strapp walked off. Then she pulled out her keys and opened the art room door so Liza could drop off her portfolio.

It sounded so funny hearing Ms. Young being called Emily, and Mr. Strapp being called Chas. I mean, I know teachers have first names, but it sounds so weird hearing them use them.

Just then, the first warning bell sounded. I had to get to my English class on the other side of the school, which meant I had to hurry. My teacher, Ms. Jaffe (I don't even know *her* first name!), gets really angry when you're late to class.

"See you later, Liza," I said as I turned and hurried off.

"Bye, Jen," Liza answered. "And thanks again!"

Liza was still in a good mood when she and I climbed on the school bus along with Chloe that afternoon. The minute Chloe had heard Liza was coming over to meet my aunt, she'd basically invited herself to come with us. Chloe really wanted to meet my aunt Amy because her dream is to live in New York one day. She wanted to hear all about the city. And I couldn't say no to Chloe when I'd already said yes to Liza. Besides, I thought my aunt would really like Chloe.

"How many Broadway shows has your aunt Amy seen?" Chloe asked me excitedly as the bus pulled out of the parking lot.

I shrugged. "I don't know. She's lived in New York a long time, so probably a lot," I told her.

"Maybe one day she'll buy tickets to see me in a Broadway show," she said.

"If you're in one, I'll make sure she goes to see it," I assured Chloe.

"What do you mean *if*?" Chloe demanded.

I had to admire Chloe's self-confidence. "Sorry," I apologized. "Of course I mean *when* you're in a show."

"That's better," Chloe said with a laugh. But I could tell she was only half joking. She looked over at Liza. "You're awfully quiet."

Liza shrugged. "I'm a little nervous, I guess."

"Of what?" Chloe asked. "Meeting Jenny's aunt?"

"Not because she's Jenny's aunt, but because she's an art director," Liza explained. "What if she thinks I don't have any talent?"

"She won't think that," I assured her. "You have a lot of talent. And she'll be able to tell you what to work on to get even better."

Liza smiled at me. "I hope you're right," she said.

"I know I am," I replied. "Aunt Amy is going to go crazy for your artwork."

Or at least she would if Chloe ever let her look at it. From the minute my friends and I walked into the house, Chloe took center stage. She wasn't letting Liza get a word in edgewise. Or me, either, for that matter.

For a while Liza and I were pretty patient. But eventually I could tell Liza's nerves were getting the better of her. I was afraid she was just going to go home without ever showing Aunt Amy her sketchbook. And there was no way I was going to let that happen.

"Um . . . Chloe," I said, interrupting her attempt to sing the entire score of the show *Wicked* for my aunt. "You want to come upstairs and play with the mice for a while?"

"Now?" Chloe asked me.

"Yeah. Now would be good," I said. "That way Liza and Aunt Amy can talk about art for a while."

"But I was just about to . . ." Chloe began. Then she caught my eye. She must have gotten the hint, because she stopped talking. "Oh. Okay," she said after a moment. Then she turned to my aunt. "You're going to be here for a few more days. I'll sing for you another time."

"I can't wait," my aunt replied with a smile. She looked at Liza. "Jenny tells me you're a good artist," she said.

"I said she was a *great* artist," I corrected her.

"Sorry," Aunt Amy said. "How about you go upstairs with Chloe and leave the great artist and me alone to talk, okay?"

I really would have loved to have heard everything my aunt had to say to Liza, but I knew I couldn't just hang out there and eavesdrop, especially now that I'd sent Chloe up to my room. It wouldn't have been very fair of me to leave her up there all by herself. It wouldn't have been fair to my mice, either. Chloe had a habit of letting them loose by mistake. I didn't want to have to spend the rest of the afternoon searching under beds and in closets for them.

"Okay," I agreed as I headed toward the stairs. "See you both later."

Chapter
FOUR

"I CAN'T BELIEVE how long Liza and your aunt spent together yesterday afternoon," Chloe said to me the next morning when we met up in the parking lot before school. "They were still looking at that sketchbook when I went home for dinner."

I didn't know what to say. Chloe actually sounded like she was jealous that Aunt Amy had spent more time with Liza than with her. But Liza and my aunt had been talking about the art business. And Chloe . . . well . . . Chloe had been talking about Chloe.

"So what did your aunt think of Liza's drawings?" Chloe asked me.

"Ask her yourself," I replied, pointing toward Liza, who was hurrying over to where Chloe and I were standing.

"Hi, guys," Liza said as she reached us.

"Hi," I said.

"You sure look like you're in a good mood," Chloe said. "I guess Jenny's aunt liked your sketches."

Liza blushed a little. "She liked some of them," she said.

Of all my friends, Liza is the one that brags the least, which is why her last sentence was the understatement of the year. "Aunt Amy didn't just like your drawings, she *loved* them," I corrected Liza.

Liza smiled shyly.

"And she wants her to come over again this evening with some more," I continued.

"My mom said she would drop me off at your house after I finish sketching Rachel and Felicia this afternoon," Liza told me.

"Oh, cool," Chloe said. "Maybe I'll come by, too."

Liza got a panicky look in her eyes, but she didn't say anything. She's too nice to ever tell someone that she'd rather he or she not tag along. So it was up to me to rescue Liza (and my aunt) from having Chloe monopolize the evening.

"The thing is, Chloe, this is kind of a business meeting," I told her. "Just the two of them. And I have homework to do tonight, so you can't really hang out in my room with me, either."

Chloe considered that for a minute. Then she said, "Yeah, I guess I should probably do homework tonight, too. We have that Spanish quiz coming up."

"Exactly," I agreed.

"Besides, Bingo misses me when I don't come right home after school to play with him. He's getting really amazing at fetch," Chloe continued. "And you should see him roll over!"

I grinned. Chloe was really crazy about her dog. The way she talked about him it was like he was some sort of canine Einstein or something.

"But I can come over *tomorrow* night," Chloe continued. "That's Friday night, so it's not like we'll have anything due the next day. I never do homework on Friday nights. It's against the rules."

"Which rules?" I asked.

"*My* rules," Chloe said with a laugh.

I had no idea Chloe had her own set of middle school rules. I wondered what number rule she was up to. Regardless, it was an excellent rule. No one should have to do homework on a Friday. Fridays are for fun!

"How about if you sleep over tomorrow night?" I suggested.

"If my folks say yes, I'm there," Chloe said.

"Me, too," Liza said.

Chloe looked a little bummed. "You're going to hang out at Jenny's today *and* tomorrow?" she asked Liza.

I could tell that Liza was a little hurt by that. Sometimes Chloe doesn't stop to think about how the things she says affect other people. She's not mean, she just says whatever she's thinking. And

166977

in this case, that meant I had to put one of my own unwritten middle school rules into effect.

MIDDLE SCHOOL RULE #39:

DO WHATEVER YOU CAN TO STOP YOUR FRIENDS FROM ARGUING OR HURTING ONE ANOTHER. KEEPING THE PEACE WILL KEEP YOU FROM BEING CAUGHT IN THE MIDDLE OF THEIR FIGHTS.

"Liza's not really hanging out tonight," I quickly reminded Chloe. "She's getting artistic advice. Tomorrow she'll be hanging out — with us."

Liza smiled gratefully at me. I smiled back.

"That sounds cool," Chloe agreed.

At just that moment, the bell rang. "Come on, Chloe," I said. "We have to hurry if we're going to get to our lockers before English."

Chloe nodded in agreement. "I have to be on time today," she said. "If I'm late one more time, Ms. Jaffe is going to make me have a silent lunch in the office. I hate sitting all by myself and not talking for a whole lunch period."

I sighed. Knowing Chloe as well as I did, I could only imagine that a silent lunch would be nothing short of torture for her.

*   *   *

I didn't have any meetings that afternoon, so I went home right after school. My mother, aunt, and I had big plans. It was Monopoly Thursday. I know that sounds kind of strange, but it's sort of a tradition. Whenever my aunt Amy comes to visit, we have a Monopoly day. The three of us sit in our kitchen and play on the old Monopoly game board my mother had when she was a girl. I'm always the race car. My aunt Amy is always the shoe. And my mother likes to be the dog.

We're not a particularly competitive family. At least not usually. But when it comes to Monopoly, it's a whole other story. You wouldn't believe how excited my mom gets when someone lands on Boardwalk. Especially if she's already got a hotel or a few houses sitting on it. She goes absolutely wacko when she starts demanding her money. Sometimes I'm tempted to film our games so I can post a video of my mom on the Internet.

However, I was the one who was celebrating when the doorbell rang late that afternoon. Aunt Amy had just landed on Marvin Gardens, which I happened to own. She owed me a ton of money, and I couldn't wait to collect.

"Come on, fork over the cash," I said greedily.

"Hang on, millionairess," Aunt Amy replied. "I have to count up the money."

"I'll get the door while you two figure out the high finance," my mom teased. A moment later she called out, "Jenny! Liza's here."

I'd almost forgotten Liza was coming over. The game had been so exciting, I'd pretty much blocked out everything else that was going on. But that was okay. Now my friend could watch me demolish my mother and her sister in a killer game of Monopoly. Judging by the size of the pile of cash in front of me, and the measly paper dollars in front of where my mom and aunt were sitting, it wouldn't be long now.

"Come on in, Liza," I said. "Take a seat. I'm totally killing them."

"Hi, Liza," Aunt Amy greeted her. "Did you bring the sketches?"

Liza nodded. "I brought some really funny dog pictures, and one of the lion I drew on our baseball caps for Spirit Week. You remember, don't you, Jenny?"

"Yeah. They were awesome." I turned my attention to Aunt Amy. "Um, I believe you owe me some cash."

Aunt Amy frowned slightly. "Sorry, kiddo. But Liza and I have plans to look over some sketches." She turned to Liza. "Did you bring the ones you did of your friends, too?"

Liza nodded "Not the actual paintings, of course. Just the sketches I made."

"That's perfect. I want to look at both because I'm not sure whether I'd want to put kids or animals on the cards." Aunt Amy glanced over at my mom and me. "I'm thinking we might be able to use one or two of Liza's drawings on greeting cards," she explained.

My mother's eyes opened wide. "Wow!" she exclaimed. "Liza, that's fantastic!"

"I thought it might be fun to have a line of cards designed and drawn by kids," my aunt explained. "We'd start with Liza's, and then maybe have a contest to pick some other artists to draw for the line."

"Don't you think that's a great idea, Jenny?" my mother asked me.

"Sure," I agreed. "But do you have to work on that now? I mean, another few moves, and I'll have beaten you."

"My mom is going to pick me up in an hour," Liza told me. "I have a lot of homework."

"So does Jenny," my mother told her. She turned toward me. "Why don't you go upstairs and get going on that Spanish vocabulary list of yours?"

I sighed heavily. We'd never stopped a Monopoly game in the middle before, ever. This was the first time. I was not happy about it.

But seeing the excited look on Liza's face made it impossible for me to argue with my mom and aunt. What Aunt Amy and Liza had to discuss was much more important than any game. And besides, I was the one who had introduced my aunt to my friend. So I couldn't really be angry, could I?

And I wasn't angry. Really, I wasn't. In fact, things between Liza and me were great the next evening when she, Chloe, and I went to the movie theater as part of our sleepover. My parents and Aunt Amy were visiting some friends, so Chloe's mom agreed to take us to the movie and then bring us to my house afterward for the sleepover.

I'm not allowed to go to the movies alone yet. And Chloe and Liza aren't, either. So Chloe's mom was going to see the movie, too. Only she was going to sit somewhere else in the theater, far enough from us so that it looked like we were there by ourselves. I thought that was an excellent plan. I wouldn't want to bump into the Pops while I was sitting with Chloe's mom. Most of the Pops are already allowed to go to the movies by themselves.

Luckily, I didn't see Addie, Dana, Maya, or any of the other Pops at the theater when we got there. That was definitely a relief. It would be a lot easier to enjoy the movie if I didn't have to keep wondering if they were going to spot Chloe's mom in the crowd. That was one embarrassment spared.

But another mortifying moment soon leaped in to take its place. My friends and I were standing in the line for the popcorn when Chloe gasped.

"Wow, you guys, look who's here!" she exclaimed.

I turned my head to see.

"Don't look!" Chloe insisted.

"But you just *told* me to look," I reminded her.

"I know, but don't be so obvious," she replied. "They'll see you."

"*Who'll* see us?" Liza asked.

"Ms. Young and Mr. Strapp," Chloe said. "They're over there by the butter dispenser. Mr. Strapp is putting butter on his popcorn."

Now Liza and I had to turn around and stare. We couldn't help ourselves. It was too weird. Not that Mr. Strapp put butter on his popcorn – I do that, too. It was weird that our teachers were at the movie theater together.

"What are they doing here?" I asked.

"My guess is seeing a movie," Liza said with a giggle.

"But here?" I asked. "Where all of us go?"

"I know what you mean," Chloe agreed.

"I don't," Liza insisted. "What's wrong with two people going to a movie at a movie theater?"

"It's not just any two people," Chloe explained. "It's two teachers. And they're together . . . again."

Chloe was right. Mr. Strapp and Ms. Young had been together an awful lot lately. Maybe there was something to her theory about them dating.

I crossed my fingers and hoped that Ms. Young and Mr. Strapp wouldn't see us. If they did, they'd probably feel like they had to say hello – in front of everyone, including the other kids our age who were in the popcorn and candy line.

Luckily, our teachers didn't seem to notice us. Instead, they took their popcorn and sodas and headed into Theater 8 to see the movie *House on Death Street*. I'd seen ads for that movie on TV. It looked really creepy and bloody. That seemed like a weird movie for teachers to go see. I always thought they went to sophisticated foreign movies where the actors all talk in French and there are English subtitles at the bottom of the screen.

I was really relieved a few minutes later when Liza, Chloe, and I were in our seats – three rows behind Chloe's mom – and the lights in the theater went down. I could sit there in the dark with two of my very best friends, enjoying the comedy we'd come to see. Now that the lights were out, no one would be able to see us, and we couldn't see anyone. No more embarrassing moments. At least not for the next one hour and forty-three minutes.

Chapter
FIVE

"HOW WAS THE MOVIE?" my mother asked about two hours later as Chloe, Liza, and I walked into our living room after the movie.

"It was pretty good," I said.

"*Pretty* good?" Chloe asked. "It was awesome. I loved the scene where the dog was running through the market and he knocked over the oranges. Did you see the look on that guy's face?" And with that she opened her mouth wide and made her eyes bug out. She looked just like the actor in the movie.

Liza and I began to laugh hysterically. "Chloe, you crack me up," Liza told her.

Chloe grinned and took a deep bow.

"Do you girls want some cookies?" my mom asked us. "Or did you eat too much popcorn at the movies?"

"There's always room for cookies," Chloe told her.

"That's what I figured," my mom said with a grin.

We all followed my mother into the kitchen.

There were already three glasses of milk and a plate of cookies on the table. I guess my mom had already suspected that we were going to want chocolate chip cookies when we got home.

My friends and I had just sat down at the table when Aunt Amy came into the kitchen with a large, overstuffed, beige-colored envelope. "Hi, girls," she greeted us.

"Hi, Aunt Amy," I replied. "We saw a funny movie tonight. You'd love it."

"She doesn't need to go to the movie," Liza said. "Chloe can act it out for her. Chloe, do the look on that guy's face again."

Chloe did not have to be asked twice. She was always ready for a performance. So once again, she opened her mouth wide and made her eyes bug out. Then, for extra measure, she let out a deep, "What the . . . AAAAAHHHH!" just like the guy had done in the movie.

Aunt Amy laughed heartily. "Chloe, you're destined for stardom," she assured my friend.

Chloe smiled happily. That was just the kind of compliment she loved.

Aunt Amy turned her attention to Liza. "This package is for you," she told her. "I had them send it from the New York office."

Now that got my attention. Why was *my* aunt giving *Liza* a present? Chloe must have wondered the same thing, because she shot me a look across the table.

"It's some cards we've already put out," Aunt Amy continued. "I figured you might get some inspiration from them." She reached in and pulled out a card with a dog in a Santa hat on the front. "This one was a big seller. When you push this button, you hear a dog barking 'Jingle Bells.'"

Chloe and I didn't say much after that. We just ate our cookies and listened as Aunt Amy and Liza discussed color choices, and which cards were the most popular.

They were so engrossed in their conversation that neither one of them seemed to notice when Chloe and I got up, put our dishes in the sink, and went upstairs to my room.

"Well that was obnoxious," Chloe said as she plopped down on my bed.

Ordinarily, I would have defended Aunt Amy and Liza. I always try to see the good in people. But I actually thought they'd been rude, too. Really rude.

"Liza's acting differently since she's been discovered," Chloe continued.

"'Discovered'?" I repeated, not sure what she meant.

"You know, since your aunt discovered her and is going to turn her into a professional artist,"

Chloe explained. "Liza should be more grateful to you. After all, you're the one who introduced her to your favorite aunt and all."

I thought about that for a minute. Liza had been very grateful to me. At least at first. But now she was kind of ignoring me. And she'd basically stolen my favorite aunt from me. Well, okay, not literally. But Aunt Amy had always spent a lot of time hanging out with me during her visits. And now she was downstairs hanging out with Liza. To top it all off, Liza didn't seem to care if my feelings were hurt by that at all. Chloe was right. Liza had changed.

"I don't want to talk about Liza anymore," I said honestly.

"Me, neither," Chloe agreed. "I want to talk about Ms. Young and Mr. Strapp. How bizarre was that?"

"Megabizarre," I agreed.

"Do you think he put his arm around her during the scary parts of the movie?" Chloe asked me. "Do you think she buried her head in his shoulder so she didn't have to see the blood and guts?"

"I don't want to think about it at all," I told Chloe as I shuddered slightly.

Chloe laughed. "I know what you mean," she said.

Just then, Liza appeared in my doorway, clutching her package of greeting cards. "What's so funny?" she asked.

Chloe and I stopped laughing. "We were just talking about Ms. Young and Mr. Strapp. Pretty creepy, huh?"

"I don't think it's creepy at all," Liza said. "I think it's nice."

"You would," Chloe told her.

"What's that supposed to mean?" Liza asked.

"It's just that you're Ms. Young's pet," Chloe explained. "So naturally, you're going to think anything she does is nice."

"That's not true," Liza said. "I'm not a teacher's pet."

I shook my head. "Come on, Liza, you know you're Ms. Young's favorite."

"Ms. Young doesn't have a favorite," Liza insisted. "She's not that kind of teacher."

Chloe shook her head. "She's never going to admit it, Jenny," she said. "We're going to have to give her scientific proof."

"How would you do that?" I asked Chloe.

"Middleschoolsurvival.com," Chloe said. "I'm sure they have some quiz that proves whether or not you're a teacher's pet."

"Great idea!" I exclaimed. Then I went over to my computer and logged on to our favorite website. I scrolled down the list of quizzes until I found what I was searching for. "Yep, here's a teacher's pet quiz you can take, Liza."

"Unless you're afraid to find out if you're really Ms. Young's pet," Chloe teased.

Liza scrunched up her mouth slightly. I could tell she felt cornered. Part of me wanted to just turn off the computer and forget about the whole thing. But part of me was still mad about how she had treated Chloe and me down in the kitchen.

"Sure," Liza said finally. "I'll take the quiz. But you guys are going to feel really silly when you find out I'm not the teacher's pet."

"Oh, I don't think that's going to happen," Chloe said. "Start reading the quiz, Jenny."

I did.

Are You a Teacher's Pet?

Every class has a teacher's pet. You can spot them pretty easily. They're the kid who the teacher always calls on when it's time to do something special. And they're the kid who gets all the praise and glory. Some kids really want to be the teacher's pet. Others are totally not interested. How about you? How important is it that your teachers treat you specially?

1. You hear it's your favorite teacher's birthday. What do you do?

A. Wish him a happy birthday on the way out of class.

B. Make him a card.

C. Nothing at all. It's not a federal holiday or anything.

Liza thought about that for a moment. "That question's not really fair," she said finally. "I mean, Ms. Young is an art teacher. We all made her birthday cards in the art room."

"*All* of you?" Chloe asked. "Was that a seventh grade thing? Because none of the sixth graders made her cards."

Liza looked questioningly over toward me.

I shrugged. "I don't actually know when her birthday is," I admitted. "So I definitely didn't make her a card."

"I didn't even wish her a happy birthday," Chloe pointed out.

"Well, I made her a card on her birthday," Liza said. "So it's B."

I clicked the mouse over the letter B and watched as the next question in the quiz popped onto the screen.

2. **You arrive at your favorite class and discover a substitute teacher in the front of the room. What is your reaction?**

A. Awesome! It's party time in the classroom.
B. You're relieved because you have an extra night to fix last night's homework.
C. You're totally bummed. You looked forward to this class all day.

I already knew the answer to that question. I remembered how upset Liza had been the other morning when she thought Ms. Young was going to be absent. So I wasn't at all surprised when she said, "That one is definitely C."

The next question appeared.

3. Where do you sit in the classroom?

    A. Right up in the front row.

    B. In the middle row, off to the side.

    C. In the back row.

"It's an art room," Liza said. "There are no rows. But I do sit off to the side, near the windows. I like the light there."

"Okay, then it's B," Chloe said.

"Yeah," Liza agreed.

4. Your teacher has asked for volunteers to help with the next school assembly. What do you do?

    A. Wait to see which of your friends are volunteering before you do.

    B. Raise your hand immediately.

    C. You don't raise your hand. You're not the volunteer type.

"That's B," Liza said. "But not because I'm a teacher's pet. I just love to do art, and any opportunity I get, I volunteer. But that's the only class I do that in."

The next question popped up on the screen. I read it out loud to Liza and Chloe.

5. Your teacher makes a corny joke. How do you react?

    A. Burst out laughing — this teacher totally cracks you up.

    B. Laugh a little. After all, you don't want to hurt her feelings.

    C. Roll your eyes and go back to writing a note to your friend in the seat next to you.

"That's B, I guess," Liza said. "Ms. Young is really nice, and cool, but she's not so funny."

"B it is," I said, clicking the button.

A new screen popped up on the computer.

That was our last question. Now it's time to total up your score:

1. A) 2	B) 1	C) 3
2. A) 3	B) 2	C) 1
3. A) 1	B) 2	C) 3
4. A) 2	B) 1	C) 3
5. A) 1	B) 2	C) 3

You scored 7 points. What does your score say about your relationship with your teachers?

5-8 points: You are definitely a teacher's pet. There's nothing you wouldn't do to impress your favorite teacher. It's nice that there's a teacher you have a good relationship with, but remember, it's important to get good grades and take part in school events for your own sake, not just to make a teacher proud of you.

9-12 points: You're not a teacher's pet, but you do behave in a way that will make your teachers respect you.

13-15 points: Okay, you've proven your point. You don't care if you are favored by any of your teachers. But just because being a teacher's pet isn't important to you, there's no excuse for being disrespectful, or not taking your school responsibilities seriously.

"Well, that settles it," Chloe said smugly. "You are totally Ms. Young's pet."

Liza didn't say anything. She kind of sat there, looking at the computer screen. I started to feel sorry for her. We were all supposed to be having a fun time tonight, and Chloe and I had ganged up on her and forced her to take this quiz. That wasn't really fair.

"You guys want to watch another movie?" I asked, shutting down the computer and trying to change the subject. "Maybe a scary one? Or a funny one?"

"How about a really old movie?" Chloe said. "Don't your parents have a whole collection of black-and-white movies?"

Liza seemed to like that idea. "Oh, I love old movies. Everything always turns out okay in the end."

"I like that, too," I agreed. "Let's go downstairs and take over the TV and the DVD player."

As my friends and I headed out of my room toward the stairs, I began to feel better. Now we were all having a great time again. This was what I had planned.

But Aunt Amy met us in the hallway. She was carrying a few more greeting cards in her hand. "Perfect timing," she said.

"You want to watch an old movie with us?" I asked her.

Aunt Amy shook her head. "I'm kind of tired. I was just bringing these up to show Liza. They're a few samples I left out of the package I gave her."

Liza looked from Chloe and me, to Aunt Amy, and back again. I could tell she didn't know what to say.

"You two girls go ahead and set up the movie,"

Aunt Amy told Chloe and me. "I'll send Liza back to you in a minute. I just want to show her these really quickly."

And just like that, my good mood disappeared again. And it was going to take a lot more than a black-and-white movie with a happy ending to bring it back.

Chapter
SIX

MONDAY AFTERNOON was a really busy time at Joyce Kilmer Middle School, especially for the kids who were part of the student council. We were responsible for helping to set up the gym for the big Career Day event. I was working alone, because most of my friends had other after-school activities to go to. But Addie had managed to recruit the "Pop Squad" (at least that's what *I* called them) to help her.

Actually, I didn't see the Pops doing any real work. Mostly they were just roaming around the gym, *pretending* to be busy while they bragged about themselves, and made fun of the people everyone else had invited.

"My mom said that Phoebe Mann, the weekend anchorwoman from the TV station, was coming tomorrow," Dana said, in a voice loud enough for everyone in the gym to hear. "I wanted Kathie Ryder, who does the weather on the six o'clock weekday news, but you know how busy weatherologists can be."

"I think you mean *meteoro*logists," Mrs. Johnson, one of our science teachers, who was helping out in the gym, told Dana. "That's what you call people who study weather."

Dana just sort of shrugged and smiled. She wasn't embarrassed at all. Now, had that been me, I would have been blushing really hard if a teacher had corrected me in front of everyone. But Dana didn't seem to care at all. In fact, she just kept babbling loudly. I cringed as she walked past the table I was preparing for my aunt Amy.

I wasn't embarrassed about the table. I actually had done a pretty nice job of decorating it. I'd made a sign that read AMY ANDREWS: ART DIRECTOR. And then I'd surrounded the words with greeting cards my aunt had given me to use. They were nice cards — not as cool as the ones she'd given Liza — but still nice. I tried not to let that bother me. But it was hard. Especially when Dana and Maya stopped to look at the table.

"Oh, an art director," Maya said. "Well, that's *sort of* interesting."

I was shocked. Coming from Maya, that was basically a compliment.

"Thanks," I said. "My aunt has a very important job."

Maya shrugged. "Not as important as Addie's

mom," she said. "Mrs. Wilson is a nurse. She saves lives."

I rolled my eyes. Did Maya really think she had to tell me what Addie's mom did for a living? I'd known Addie a whole lot longer than Maya had.

"Too bad you're working here all by yourself," Dana told me. "If your aunt is an art director, you should have had your friend Liza help you set up this table."

"Why?" I asked her.

"Isn't Liza the Leonardo DiCaprio of your group of friends?" Dana asked me.

What was she talking about? "The who?" I asked.

"Leonardo DiCaprio," Dana repeated. "You know, the famous artist."

I started to laugh. So did Maya, even though she was Dana's friend. She just couldn't help herself.

"I think you mean Leonardo *da Vinci*," I told Dana. "He was the artist. Leonardo DiCaprio is an actor."

Dana shook her head. "You are so wrong, Jenny."

Maya giggled. "Actually, she's right," she said. "Leonardo DiCaprio is an actor. He was in that old movie *Titanic*, remember?"

"Where he played an *artist*," Dana said smugly. "So I wasn't wrong after all."

Wow. In some weird alternate Pop universe, Dana had managed to make perfect sense. She'd also managed to make me feel even worse about everything that was going on in my life.

Oddly enough, I wasn't exactly sure what it was I was upset about. At least not completely. I was kind of mad at Liza because she'd totally taken my aunt's attention away from me. And I was kind of angry with my aunt for having more in common with Liza than she did with me. But mostly I think I was furious with myself for being jealous, especially since I was the one who had introduced them in the first place. I had a big, angry, sad jumble of emotions pouring through me, and having to listen to Dana blab on and on about it didn't help. So I just walked away, leaving Dana and Maya to stare at the table I had prepared for Aunt Amy.

I didn't care about being rude to Dana and Maya. For one thing, they're Pops, which means they're plenty rude a lot of the time. And secondly, I didn't have time to stand around talking about either Leonardo. I had responsibilities. For instance, I needed to make sure that everything was set up for the twins' parents when they arrived tomorrow. I had arranged for them to have an extra-large table. I had a feeling a lot of kids were going to be stopping by to hear what it was like to own a bakery — especially since Marilyn and Carolyn had made sure that their parents were coming with enough minicupcakes for the whole school! I was pretty sure no one would be able to resist that.

I was right. The free cupcakes meant that the bakery table was mobbed from the moment Career Day started. So was the table where Marc's father was sitting. He was giving away free sweatbands and miniposters of famous athletes.

Boy, did that make Addie Wilson mad! She was not pleased that free cupcakes and sweatbands were a whole lot more interesting to kids than blowing into a resuscitation doll was. "Jenny, your friends are really sneaky," Addie snarled at me as we passed each other on the way to different tables in the gym. "They had their parents bring things to give away just so their tables would be the most popular."

I rolled my eyes. "Addie, not everything is a popularity contest," I insisted.

Addie didn't answer me. I figured that was because she thought I was nuts. To her (and to the other Pops), everything *was* a popularity contest. And the fact that there was a longer line at Marc's dad's table than at her mom's was really making her furious.

Still, there was a little part of me that knew how she felt. I was really glad that there was a steady flow of kids visiting my aunt Amy's table. Plenty of kids seemed interested in hearing about how greeting cards were made and what it was like to be an art director at a big company. At least that's what I figured Aunt Amy was telling the kids that stopped by to talk to her. I actually hadn't gone over to her table to hear what she was saying.

I'd been to some of the other tables in the gym, though. I'd already gone over to talk to a woman who was a kindergarten teacher. That was something I was really thinking seriously about doing when I grew up. I told her about the mentoring program my friends and I do with little kids at the elementary school on Thursdays, and she gave me some ideas for art projects I could do with the kids, which was really helpful.

After talking to the kindergarten teacher, I'd let Chloe drag me over to meet a man who did the voices for cartoon shows on TV. That was more interesting for her than it was for me, so I left and headed toward the table Sandee had set up for her mom and the mayor. I thought it would be really cool to meet the person who was in charge of our town's government. But before I could get anywhere near the mayor's table I ran into Marilyn and Carolyn.

"Hey, Jenny," Carolyn greeted me.

"Having fun?" Marilyn asked.

"Oh, yeah," I told the twins. "This is really awesome."

"Any day we have a break from two of our afternoon classes is okay with me," Carolyn said.

"Me, too," Marilyn agreed.

"Seriously," I agreed. "I needed the break, big-time!"

"You know who else is having a fun day?" Carolyn asked me.

I shook my head.

"Ms. Young," Carolyn said.

"And Mr. Strapp," Marilyn added. "Have you seen the way they keep looking at each other?"

I shook my head. "Not you guys, too," I groaned. "We don't even know if they're really dating. Chloe just made that up."

"I don't think so," Marilyn said.

"They keep staring at each other," Carolyn added.

I glanced over toward the corner of the gym, where Ms. Young was standing. She was staring off into space with a kind of goofy smile on her face. As I followed the direction of her gaze, I noticed she was looking across the gym at Mr. Strapp. And he was looking back at her with the same goofy smile.

"Wow," I said quietly.

"I know," Marilyn said.

"They're totally into each other," Carolyn added.

"Do you think Liza will be a junior brides-maid if they get married?" Marilyn asked her sister and me.

"She and Ms. Young are really close," Carolyn said. "They have that whole love-of-art thing in common."

I rolled my eyes. Was Liza all anyone could talk about these days?

"I doubt any students would be invited to the wedding," I told the twins.

"What wedding?" Chloe asked as she, Felicia, and Rachel came over to where the twins and I were standing.

"Ms. Young and Mr. Strapp's wedding," Carolyn and Marilyn told her.

"They got engaged?" Chloe asked excitedly.

Uh-oh. I knew once Chloe got something like that into her head, there would be no stopping her. The whole school would hear about it in the time it took to hit *send* on a mass e-mail. I had to stop her right now.

"No," I assured her. "We were just talking about how cool it would be *if* two teachers got married. But I didn't see a diamond ring on Ms. Young's finger or anything."

"Maybe they haven't picked it out yet," Chloe said. "They could still be engaged."

"Speaking of getting engaged . . ." Rachel said with a huge grin on her face.

I'd seen that smile before. It was the one Rachel got on her face just before she told us one of her really, really bad jokes.

"What did the rabbit get his girlfriend when they got engaged?"

Felicia sighed and rolled her eyes. "What?"

"A twenty-four *carrot* gold ring!" Rachel exclaimed. Then she burst out laughing at her own joke.

I laughed a little, too, just so she wouldn't feel badly. So did the twins and Chloe. Felicia just shook her head and sighed.

"I wonder what kind of ring Mr. Strapp will buy for Ms. Young," Chloe said. "You think the diamond will be huge?"

"I doubt it," Felicia said. "I don't think teachers make a lot of money."

"They might just be friends," I reminded my friends. I didn't want rumors starting that weren't true. My friends and I had all had untrue rumors started about us at one time or another (usually by the Pops). So I knew how bad it felt to have people spread lies about you. Ms. Young and Mr. Strapp were two of the nicest teachers in the school. I didn't want people to start saying they were going out if they weren't. Although from the way they were staring at each other across the gym, I had a feeling my friends were right about the two of them.

Still, it wasn't nice to talk behind their backs. "Anyway, did you guys meet anyone interesting at this fair?" I asked, trying to change the subject.

"Too bad there isn't a wedding planner here today," Chloe said.

I sighed. When Chloe got an idea in her head she just would not let it go. She was like a dog with a bone. No wonder she loved Bingo so much. They had a lot in common.

"No, but the mayor is at that table over there," I said, pointing toward the far left corner end of the gym. "That's where I was heading. I'd like to meet her."

"Okay," Chloe said. "I'll go with you."

In order to get to the mayor's table, Chloe and I had to pass by my aunt. Even though I was still upset with Aunt Amy for spending so much time with Liza instead of me, I didn't want to be completely rude, so I turned and waved as we walked by. My aunt waved back. I was kind of surprised to see a few of the Pops standing around her table. Addie, Dana, and Claire were all there, listening with rapt interest to what makes a successful greeting card. Talk about bizarre. What interest would the Pops have in greeting cards? It's not like Aunt Amy was giving away free makeup. She wasn't even giving away free *greeting cards.*

But my curiosity about the Pops' sudden interest in cards was interrupted as Marc suddenly jumped up in front of us with his camera in hand. "Give me a smile for the yearbook," he said.

"I thought yearbook pictures were taken a few weeks ago," I replied.

"Those were the individual and club shots," Marc explained. "But we keep taking pictures of events like these all year, so we can get as many in the yearbook as possible," he said.

"Have you been taking pictures all day?" I asked him. "Didn't you get to talk to any of the visitors?"

"I did the whole Career Day thing last year," Marc explained. "Besides, I already know what career I'm headed for."

I smiled. We *all* knew what career Marc was going to pursue.

"Smile for the camera," Marc told Chloe and me.

We wrapped our arms around each other's shoulders, and I forced a huge smile to my face. No sense in having the fact that I was kind of unhappy about the whole Aunt Amy-Liza thing go down in history. I'd probably feel better about it in a day or two, anyway. I didn't want a reminder of it right there in black-and-white every time I opened the yearbook.

That afternoon, my aunt gave me a ride home in the car she'd rented to use while she was visiting us. I smiled as I climbed into the front seat and buckled up. The car had that wonderful new-car scent. My family's cars usually smelled like stale french fries and pine air fresheners, so this was a real treat for me.

"You have some really nice friends," Aunt Amy said as she put the key in the ignition. "It was wonderful seeing Addie again. You sure you don't want to give her a ride home?"

I sighed. The last time Aunt Amy had come to town, I'd still been in elementary school, which meant Addie had still been my best friend. I didn't feel like going into the whole Addie-leaving-me-for-the-Pops story with her. For some reason, adults always seem to think that it's possible for everyone in middle school to be friends. I don't know if that's because it was that way when they were in middle school, or if they've just forgotten what it was like, but they're always convinced that groups in middle school can blend easily. I really didn't want to hear a whole lecture on the importance of old friends like Addie Wilson from my aunt. So I just said,

"Addie likes the bus. She wouldn't want to go home in a car."

My aunt looked at me curiously, but she didn't say anything. Instead, she turned the key and we drove off in silence. At least it was silent for a little while. But then my aunt started to make conversation. "It's nice the way your old friends, like Addie and Dana, are so chummy with your new friends, like Liza."

I rolled my eyes. Obviously I hadn't avoided the subject after all. "Addie and Dana aren't friends with Liza," I told my aunt.

"Really?" she replied. "They seemed friendly when they were all hanging around at my Career Day table. The girls seemed so interested in Liza's artwork."

I sighed heavily. I knew they were just acting interested because there was an adult around. The Pops were very good at pretending to be nice. But the minute the adult in the room disappeared, they always went back to being the mean Pops they usually were.

"I was kind of surprised *you* didn't stop by the table," Aunt Amy continued.

I shrugged. "I already know all about your job," I told her. "I wanted to talk to people about jobs I found interesting, like the kindergarten teacher and the mayor."

"You're thinking about running for mayor?" Aunt Amy asked me, obviously ignoring the fact that I'd sort of just said I didn't think her job was interesting. Which was good, because I hadn't meant it that way. Not really, anyway.

"No," I told her. "But I am sixth grade class president, so I thought I should meet her."

"One politician to another," my aunt said with a little chuckle.

"Exactly," I replied.

"Well, that's good," Aunt Amy continued. "Because I thought maybe you didn't come by because you were angry with me."

Boy, she was smart. I thought I'd been hiding that pretty well. But apparently not. Still, I wasn't ready to admit anything. "Why would I be angry?" I asked.

"Because we had to stop the Monopoly game the other day," Aunt Amy said. "You haven't been the same since then."

That definitely stopped me in my tracks. I had been plenty mad about the game ending early. I guess I hadn't hidden it at all.

I just wanted the conversation to end. If I were home I'd have made some excuse and gone upstairs to my room. But I was stuck in the car with Aunt Amy. So I changed the subject. "Can I put on the radio?" I asked her. "There's an oldies station you'd probably like."

"Ouch!" Aunt Amy exclaimed. But she was smiling. "It hurts to hear my favorite songs called oldies."

"Then do you want me to put on the Top Forty station instead?" I asked her.

"You can put on anything you want, kiddo," Aunt Amy replied. "Whatever makes you happy."

I smiled. It was nice to hear my aunt being concerned with my happiness for a change. I switched on the Top 40 radio station and settled back in my seat. As I sat there listening to one of my favorite Cody Tucker songs, I began to relax for the first time in days. I had a feeling that since the whole Career Day thing was behind us, things were going to go back to normal.

Chapter
SEVEN

AND THINGS *would* have gone back to normal, if the Pops hadn't gotten involved and messed up everything all over again.

When I walked into the cafeteria for lunch on Wednesday, I was feeling pretty good about things. For starters, I'd gotten an A- on the descriptive paragraph I'd written for English, and a B+ on the Spanish quiz I'd been studying for. Even better, the lunch menu said that today they were serving breakfast for lunch, which meant French toast, pancakes, and fruit. Breakfast is a meal even *our* school cafeteria can't mess up.

Best of all, my mom, aunt, and I had had a rematch of Monopoly the night before. And even though this time my mother had won the game, I was feeling pretty victorious myself. Aunt Amy and I had overcome our problems.

As I walked into the cafeteria, the first person I spotted was Liza. She was standing near the food line. That would have seemed perfectly normal, if there weren't Pops all around her. But there she was, with Addie and Dana on one side of her, and Sabrina, Maya, and Claire on the other. Liza looked a little overwhelmed and confused. The Pops looked extremely excited. They were all talking at the same time and waving their hands wildly. The strange thing was, they didn't appear to be teasing or taunting Liza. In fact, it looked like they were making a conscious effort to be nice to her.

I don't know why, but I'm really curious about what Pops talk about. I know it's probably not anything particularly fascinating, but for some reason, I'm interested. And today I was doubly curious because whatever they were discussing obviously affected Liza. So I sidled over toward the crowd of Pops, making sure not to get so close that they could tell I was eavesdropping. But I was still standing close enough to hear everything that was going on.

"I really think you should go with portraits of kids for your greeting cards," I overheard Dana saying.

"Definitely," Addie agreed. "Kids like to buy cards with other kids' pictures on them."

"Especially if the girl on the card looks really cool," Sabrina added. "Then the card is definitely going to be a big seller."

"I don't know," I overheard Liza say nervously. "Jenny's aunt seemed to be leaning toward having me draw really cute animals."

"But even *she* wasn't completely sure, right?" Maya said. "That's because she's an adult. We're kids. We know what kids like."

"I'd be glad to pose for one of your cards," Sabrina told Liza. "I took that modeling class at Shaw's department store last year, so I'm almost a professional model. But I would pose for you for free."

"They only taught you how to put on makeup in that class," Dana corrected her. "It didn't make you a model. Besides, I'd make a better model for a greeting card. My face is friendlier than yours."

"Are you saying *I'm* not friendly?" Sabrina demanded.

I sighed. So that was what this was all about. The Pops all wanted to be on Liza's greeting cards. No wonder they were treating her like some sort of rock star. Being a real greeting card artist was making Liza a minicelebrity at our school. And the Pops considered celebrity status at Joyce Kilmer Middle School their territory. So now they were determined to make Liza one of them.

"Why don't we talk about this over lunch?" Claire asked. "I'm starving."

"Good idea," Maya agreed. "I could definitely go for pancakes."

"Come on, Liza," Addie said. "You can sit with us today."

Suddenly I felt that old jealousy rising up inside me again. Addie had just invited Liza to sit at the Pops' table for lunch. She'd never done that for me, even though she and I had been friends way before we got to Joyce Kilmer Middle School. And even though I no longer had any desire to sit at the Pops' table for lunch (that had pretty much ended by the second week of school), it still made me mad that Liza had been invited to do just that.

Surprisingly, Liza didn't look too happy about the invitation, either. Instead, she seemed nervous and overwhelmed. Then she caught a glimpse of me out of the corner of her eye.

"Hi, Jenny!" she shouted loudly so that I could hear her over all the plates clanging and kids laughing in the cafeteria.

I glanced around for a second, pretending I was noticing Liza standing there with the Pops for the first time. "Oh," I said matter-of-factly. "Hi."

"I was just about to look for you," Liza said nervously.

"I've been standing right here," I said coldly.

"Oh, right," Liza said. She seemed confused by my coldness.

She wasn't the only one. I felt a little confused, too. It was like my emotions were just zigzagging back and forth. *I'm jealous. I'm not jealous. I'm a little jealous. I'm a lot jealous.*

Right now, the fact that the Pops wanted to sit with Liza and not me was making me *a lot* jealous. I didn't want to be a Pop or anything, but it would have been fun to have been asked, just so I could turn them down.

"I'll see you later," I said to Liza. "I'm going to get some French toast, and then I'm going to sit at our usual table."

"Have fun," Addie said. "Come on, Liza."

"I . . . um . . . I was actually going to go to the art room," Liza said. "I have a lot to do for my art show project."

"Oh, come on," Sabrina urged her. "That's amateur stuff. The greeting card is your professional job. You need it to be perfect. And we're just the people to help you with that. We know what's cool and what's not."

"Jenny, you want to start posing for me now?" Liza asked, ignoring Sabrina. "You're the only one of our group of friends I haven't drawn yet."

I sighed. "Gee, Liza, I'd like to, but I'm kind of hungry," I told her. "And I need to talk to Marc about something."

"Oh," Liza said quietly. "After school, then?"

I shook my head. "I'm busy all week. I have a lot of student council stuff to do, and then I have a paper to write for history."

"But the art show is on Friday," Liza insisted. "If I don't sketch you today, and paint tomorrow, your picture won't be part of it."

"I'm sorry, Liza," I said. "But I don't think I have time to pose for your project."

I felt kind of bad when I said that. I knew I was breaking my own Middle School Rule #38. After all, I had promised to help Liza with a project. But somehow that didn't seem to matter to me at the moment.

Besides, Liza had plenty of volunteers to take my place. "I'll pose for you!" Sabrina volunteered excitedly. "It would be good practice for the greeting card." She shifted her weight to her back leg and tipped her head back in what I think was her imitation of a professional model.

"*I'll* pose for you," Dana insisted. "I have the prettiest new pink sweater. It would add a lot of color to your project."

"I already have the whole thing planned," Liza told the Pops. "And Jenny's picture is part of the plan."

I shrugged. "It looks like you have plenty of people to take my place. It doesn't really matter who you put in there. You just have to fill a hole in the display, right?"

Liza just looked at me for a minute. Then she turned to the Pops. "I . . . um . . . I have to go," she said suddenly. Then she darted out of the cafeteria.

I felt pretty crummy all day. And things didn't get better when I got home and passed by the guest bedroom. The door was open, and I could see that my aunt Amy was sitting on her bed, looking over some papers for her trip to China. I really didn't feel like spending another minute hearing how incredibly talented Liza was, and since that was about all my aunt or anyone else seemed to be able to discuss lately, I hurried silently past the guest bedroom.

But my aunt spotted me, anyway. "Hi, Jenny," Aunt Amy called out. "Good day at school?"

"For some people," I grumbled. "Just not for me."

"Pop quiz or something?" Aunt Amy asked.

I shook my head. "Nah. I'm just in a rotten mood."

"Oh," my aunt said understandingly. "I get in those, too, sometimes. You're grumpy, but you have no idea why, right?"

Wrong. I knew exactly why I was grumpy.

"I was thinking maybe on your next vacation, you could come to the city and visit me," Aunt Amy continued. "It would be so much fun, hanging out just the two of us. We didn't get to do enough of that this time around."

I looked at her with surprise. I had no idea she felt that way.

Aunt Amy laughed. "What? You didn't think I noticed we hardly got to talk?"

I didn't – *couldn't* – say anything.

"I got all caught up in business. It was great, but it wasn't what I'd planned at all," she explained.

"Me, neither," I told her.

"But I was kind of hoping you'd understand about that," Aunt Amy continued. "My job is really important to me, and this line of cards by kids could be huge. Also, I know that art is pretty much the only thing that makes Liza feel good about herself, and I figured you'd want me to help out your friend."

"How'd you know that about Liza?" I wondered. "You just met her."

"I kind of *was* her, in middle school," Aunt Amy explained.

I looked at her curiously. "What do you mean, you *were* her?"

Aunt Amy sighed heavily, and for a moment, she seemed a little sad. "I wasn't a great student. I had a tough time with some of my classes. But the one thing I could do was draw. And that made me feel special," she explained.

"Just like Liza," I said.

"Exactly," Aunt Amy replied. "I understand her in a way you and your friends might not be able to, so I wanted to help her. And she's definitely helping me. The president of the card company is really psyched about this new line of cards. It could get me a promotion."

"I'm so glad," I said. And I really meant it.

"Me, too," she replied. "And it's all thanks to you."

"To me?" I was kind of surprised to hear that.

"Sure," my aunt replied. "If you hadn't introduced me to Liza, none of this would have happened."

That sounded so odd. I'd been thinking the same thing – just not in such a positive way. I'd only been seeing the bad side of things. But obviously, I'd helped out two people I really cared about, which was pretty cool.

And just like that, my bad mood disappeared. I was suddenly feeling really good about things. It's kind of incredible how that happens sometimes.

That night, I sat in the guest room surrounded by piles of greeting cards. Aunt Amy said she wasn't going to need them when she was in China, and she thought I might want to have them. The cards were really beautiful, but I wasn't sure what I would do with them. There were a ton of them. And while I had a lot of friends, each of my friends only had a birthday once a year. I didn't know how I could use all of the cards.

"Maybe you could use them for a collage, or some sort of craft project," Aunt Amy suggested.

"That's a good idea," I said. I paused for a minute. "Do you want to do a project with me?" I asked her.

Aunt Amy smiled brightly. "You bet. What kind of project do you want to do?"

"I don't know," I admitted. "But I *do* know a place where I can get some excellent craft ideas."

"Where?" Aunt Amy asked.

"There's this amazing website," I told her. "It has everything you can imagine. I know it will have ideas for things to do with greeting cards."

"Let's check it out," Aunt Amy agreed.

A minute later, my aunt and I were sitting in front of the computer scrolling through a list of craft projects that had been posted on middleschoolsurvival.com. And naturally I found exactly what I was looking for.

Greetings . . . From Your Old Greeting Cards!
Are you one of those kids who can't throw away her old birthday cards, Christmas cards, Thanksgiving cards, Valentine's Day cards, and friendship cards? Lots of people can't bear to just

*throw away cards sent to them by their friends.
But after a while those cards start to really pile up.
That's when it's time to make a memory box. It's
the perfect place to keep memories, on the inside
and out.*

YOU WILL NEED:

- Mod Podge (a water-based glue you can find at any craft store)
- A plain, unfinished wooden box (you can find this at a craft store, too)
- An assortment of greeting cards
- A foam paintbrush
- Scissors

HERE'S WHAT YOU DO:

1. Make sure your box is free of dirt.
2. Cut out images from your greeting cards.
3. Using the foam paintbrush, apply Mod Podge glue to the box.
4. Arrange some card images in a collage over the glue on the box.
5. Brush glue over the images you glued to the box. This will seal them.
6. Keep repeating steps 3 and 5 until you have finished your design.

7. Apply a thick coat of glue over your entire design. Repeat this several times, because the more coats you put on, the thicker the finish.

"That's perfect!" Aunt Amy exclaimed. She popped up and headed toward the stairs.

"Where are you going?" I asked her.

"*We're* going to the craft store to get supplies," she replied. "You and I are going to make these boxes tonight."

"Cool," I said. "I'll get your car keys. I saw them on the counter when I came in."

"Great," Aunt Amy agreed. She paused for a minute. "Oh, and, Jenny?"

"What?" I wondered, sounding a little nervous. Was my aunt going to tell me she'd noticed that I'd been mean to Liza? I hoped not. Clearly I already knew that.

But Aunt Amy grinned. "This time, I'm choosing the radio station," she insisted.

I laughed. "Sounds fair to me," I agreed.

EIGHT

I HAD A GREAT TIME hanging out with my aunt that night. We were laughing and joking around, and it seemed as though nothing had changed. But that wasn't true. A lot had changed in the past few days, and it all had to do with my relationship with Liza. That was why by the time I got to school on Thursday morning, my good mood was gone. It had been replaced with stress and anxiety.

When I got off the bus in the school parking lot, I was hoping to bump into Liza. I was also hoping *not* to bump into Liza. I knew I needed to apologize for skipping out on my promise to be part of her art project, but I wasn't exactly sure what to say. After all, it's not exactly comfortable to tell one of your friends that you were jealous of how much time she was spending with one of your relatives — especially an adult relative. That could sound pretty dorky, even to someone who is as non-judgmental as Liza. Still, I knew I had to explain myself. Liza seemed confused about how I'd been treating her. Of course, that made sense, considering how confused I'd been about things myself.

Apparently, I was going to have plenty of time to come up with something to say to Liza, though, because when I got off the bus she was nowhere to be seen. I looked all around the parking lot – even near the back wall where the Pops usually hung out, just in case they'd kidnapped her and tried to make her one of them again. But I didn't see her anywhere. And none of my other friends seemed to have any idea where she was, either.

"She might be in the art room," Marilyn suggested.

"She spends a lot of time there these days," Carolyn added.

But Chloe shook her head. "She's not in the art room," she said.

"How do you know?" I asked her. "Have you seen her?"

"No," Chloe admitted. "But Ms. Young hasn't arrived at school yet. So there wouldn't have been anyone to unlock the room for Liza."

I looked at Chloe with surprise. "What are you, stalking Ms. Young these days?" I asked.

"What do you mean?" Chloe wondered.

"I mean, since when do you keep track of the comings and goings of the art teacher?" I explained.

"I'm not keeping track of anything," Chloe insisted. "I just think it's interesting to see if she's still carpooling with . . ." she paused dramatically for a second and then added, ". . . anyone in particular."

"*Anyone* being Mr. Strapp, perhaps?" I asked her.

Chloe giggled and then nodded. "I love stuff like this," she admitted. "It's like one of the stories in my fan magazines has come to life."

I rolled my eyes. Chloe can be such a drama queen sometimes. And while I usually find it fun to listen to her going on about one drama or another, today I had my own drama to deal with.

"They could have come in through the front door of the school," Marilyn pointed out.

"Teachers do that a lot," Carolyn agreed.

"But I don't see either of their cars in the parking lot, do you?" Chloe asked the twins.

As my friends scanned the rows of teachers' cars for one belonging to either Mr. Strapp or Ms. Young, I walked off in search of Liza. But before I could get too far, the bell rang. My apology was going to have to wait until lunch. That actually seemed pretty appropriate since when lunch rolled around, I was going to have to eat a lot of crow. That's what my mom calls it when you have to apologize for being wrong about something. And I had been *really* wrong about Liza.

*　　*　　*

The morning seemed to drag by incredibly slowly. My body was sitting in my classes, but my brain was a million miles away. Instead of listening to my teachers, I'd been practicing what I wanted to say to Liza over and over again in my head. Unfortunately, nothing I could come up with ever sounded good enough to make up for what I had done to her.

That's the problem with apologies. The words you use can never erase the actions you committed that hurt the person in the first place. But words were pretty much all I had to make this up to Liza. It was too late to pose for my portrait now.

It was also too late to think of any brilliant words of apology, since it was now lunchtime, and I was about to come face-to-face with my friend. My heart began to pound as I walked into the cafeteria. I scanned the room, looking for her, but she wasn't at our usual table, and she wasn't standing in the food line. That didn't leave many options.

"Oh, Liza, you're funny!"

My head jerked around as I heard Dana Harrison say my friend's name. I turned suddenly and spotted Liza standing in the far corner of the cafeteria — *the Pops' corner!* I gulped. Had I done something even more awful than I'd originally thought? Had my cruelty and disloyalty actually pushed Liza over the line to the Pops?

I walked cautiously over to the Pops' side of the cafeteria, trying not to be noticed. The last thing I needed was the Pops turning around and making fun of me for eavesdropping on them. I was embarrassed about enough things already.

"*Of course* you want to sit with us," Dana continued. "Everyone does."

"And you're special," Sabrina assured Liza. "That's why we've made room for you."

I stood there for a minute, waiting to hear Liza's response. But she didn't say anything. She just stood there, surrounded by Pops. She actually looked a little frightened.

I knew I had to do something. Someone had to rescue Liza from the onslaught of Pop pressure. And since I was the only one of our friends who was standing nearby, I knew I was the person to do just that.

"Liza!" I called out. "I've been looking all over for you! I need your help with . . . with . . ." I stammered for a minute, trying to think of something I would need help with. Finally I just said, ". . . with *that thing*."

It was lame, but it seemed to work. "Oh, yeah, the *thing*," Liza repeated. "I'd almost forgotten."

She turned to the Pops. "Sorry, I have to help my friend with something," she told them.

My friend. The words cut through me like a knife. I hadn't exactly been acting like Liza's friend lately. But I was going to from now on, starting with this rescue.

"Thanks, Jenny," Liza said as she made her way through the crowd of stunned Pops. I wasn't surprised that the Pops were stunned. Liza had just dissed them — not once but twice — and that was something no one else had ever done. They had to have been shocked.

"No problem," I assured her with a smile. "The Pops sure can get out of control."

"I know," Liza said. "They've been following me around all day. They all want me to draw them."

Ouch. That one really cut deep. Here the Pops had been begging Liza to draw them, and I'd begged *off* from her project. I felt worse than ever.

"Listen, Liza, I'm really sorry," I said, blurting out the words as quickly as I could. "I've been a real jerk."

Liza looked as though she'd been caught off guard. "What do you mean?" she asked me.

"The way I've been acting," I told her. "Making you take that teacher's pet quiz and not posing for your project. That was all so mean."

Liza looked at me for a minute. "It wasn't so much that it was mean," she told me. "It was more that it wasn't like you."

I wasn't sure what to say next. Liza was being so nice about this. Somehow, that was making the apology harder instead of easier.

"The thing is, I was really jealous of you," I told her. "You were spending so much time with my aunt Amy and . . ."

"But *you're* the one who introduced me to your aunt," Liza reminded me.

"I know," I told her. "And I'm not saying I had any right to be jealous. I'm just saying I was. But I'm not anymore. I'm happy for you, and I'm excited about your line of cards." I smiled as brightly as I could, just to let her know that I really meant it.

"I'm excited, too," Liza said. "This has been an incredible week for me. First your aunt asked me to draw the greeting cards, and now there's the art show tomorrow." She stopped for a minute and smiled. "I don't remember the last time I felt this happy."

I thought about what my aunt had said to me the night before, about art being the one thing that had made her feel great about herself when she had been in school. I could see that Aunt Amy had been right about Liza. From the look on her face, I could tell that was how she was feeling now, too.

"You *should* feel happy," I told Liza. "And proud. You're the best artist in the school. No one even comes close."

"Thanks, Jenny," Liza said sincerely.

"So, we're friends again?" I asked her tentatively.

Liza looked at me strangely. "We were always friends," she said. "And we always will be. Friends can go through tough times once in a while. It's no big deal."

That made me feel a lot better, for the most part. But there was still one thing that bothered me.

"I feel really badly about not posing for your project," I told her. "It's going to be special. And if it makes you feel any better, I know I'm going to feel awful tomorrow night when I see everyone else in the mural and not me."

"Oh, you're there," Liza assured me. "After all, the mural is about friendship."

"You mean I'm there in spirit?" I asked.

Liza shot me a mysterious smile. "Yeah, something like that," she replied.

Chapter

NINE

ON FRIDAY EVENING, my parents, Aunt Amy, and I
all headed over to my school for the art show. The
place was packed with kids and parents. My school
usually feels pretty huge to me. But tonight it was
definitely too small. It's amazing how much more
crowded a school can feel when the kids all have
their parents there with them.

"Let's go see your painting, Jenny," my aunt
suggested.

I flinched. I didn't exactly want to show my artwork to a real art director, even if she was my aunt.
My painting wasn't exactly what you would call a
work of art. It was more like the satisfactory com-
pletion of a middle school art class assignment.

Still, I led my parents and my aunt over to the
cafeteria, which is where most of the sixth grade
paintings had been hung. There, over by the windows, were a series of sixth grade self-portraits
done in the style of an artist named Andy Warhol.
To make my self-portrait, Ms. Young had taken a
photo of me. Then she'd blown up the photo and
copied it four times. Finally, she'd glued my four

photographs to one piece of poster board and then I'd painted them using different paint colors on each photo.

"This is really good, Jenny," my dad said proudly. "I like the one you did of yourself in all the blues and greens."

I smiled. "That's my favorite one, too," I told my dad.

"What a great assignment!" my mother exclaimed. "We never did anything like that when I was in middle school."

"No, we didn't," Aunt Amy agreed. "All we did was paint bowls of fruit."

"And trees," my mother reminded her. "Don't forget the trees."

Aunt Amy laughed. "Oh, yes. That four seasons sequence. The same tree in fall, winter, and spring."

I looked at her curiously. "I thought you said *four* seasons."

Aunt Amy nodded. "I did. But we weren't in school for summer. We were supposed to do that one on our own."

"You were the only person who did," my mother reminded her.

"That's true," Aunt Amy recalled.

"You did a lot of extra work for art class," my mother told her sister. "And when you weren't doing art projects you were painting scenery for school plays, or designing fliers for school events."

Just like Liza, I thought to myself. My aunt really wasn't kidding when she said she'd been a lot like her back in middle school.

Just then, Felicia and Josh came walking over to where my family and I were standing.

"Hi, Jenny," Felicia said. "Hi, Mr. and Mrs. McAfee."

"Hi, Ms. Andrews," Josh added.

I squirmed slightly. It always got a little uncomfortable when my friends and I were all together with our parents. We suddenly found ourselves watching our behavior and being careful about what we said. That usually led to some uncomfortable silences, like the one we were experiencing now.

It got even more uncomfortable a few seconds later, when Josh's and Felicia's parents came up behind them. Now the kids were totally outnumbered. But the adults started speaking to one another and basically ignoring us, and before long, my friends and I were talking among ourselves, which meant everything was back to being comfortable. At least it was until Felicia asked, "Have you seen Liza's special project yet?"

I shifted slightly from side to side. Even though Liza and I had made up, I still felt kind of weird about seeing her project. Being there in spirit wasn't exactly the same as seeing my face up there on the wall. And I knew I wasn't going to be the only one who noticed my missing image. My friends would all wonder what had happened, and I didn't want to have to explain over and over again what a jealous jerk I'd been.

And that would be nothing compared to explaining things to the Pops. Judging by how they had been following Liza around recently, I knew for sure they weren't going to miss checking out her project — if only to suck up to her in the hopes of having their pictures on the front of a greeting card.

Still, I did want to support Liza, especially after how I'd behaved. She'd worked hard — *really hard* — on her art show display. The least I could do was go see it and congratulate her.

"Where is it?" I asked Felicia and Josh.

"Over by the front entrance to the school," Josh said. "I don't know how you missed it when you came in."

"We came in through the cafeteria entrance," I explained. "We parked back there."

"Well, you have to go see it," Felicia urged. "It's amazing."

She was right. I had to go see it. "Mom," I called over. Then, realizing I'd interrupted her conversation, I added, "Excuse me."

My mom smiled. She always likes when I act politely. "What's up, honey?" she asked.

"Is it okay if I go over to the front hall? Liza's project is set up there."

"Sure," my mom said with a nod. "We'll meet you over there in a little bit."

"Sounds good," I agreed. I turned to Josh and Felicia. "You guys want to come with me?"

"Definitely," Felicia said.

Liza was standing right in the center of the hall when I spotted her. As I'd predicted, she was surrounded by gushing Pops. They were all standing around, *ooh*ing and *aah*ing. I couldn't even see Liza's paintings, because the Pops were blocking them from view.

"Liza, this is amazing," I heard Dana say. "You really are just like a professional."

"What do you mean 'just like'?" Claire countered. "She *is* a professional. Or she will be, as soon as she draws those greeting cards."

"Speaking of which," Addie said, "we were thinking maybe you could do a series of cards instead of just one. It could be sort of like this art exhibit, except with really amazing kids, instead of *these* kids."

"These are my friends," Liza reminded her.

"Oh, of course they are," Dana said. "But they're not right for a line of professional greeting cards. I mean, why would anyone buy a picture of Jenny McAfee, when they could buy one of, say . . . oh . . . I don't know . . . *me*, maybe?"

I rolled my eyes and groaned slightly. Dana could be so obnoxious and conceited sometimes. No, not sometimes. All of the time.

And then suddenly something hit me. Dana had just said, "a picture of Jenny McAfee." Was it possible? It couldn't be. I hadn't posed for a portrait. There was no way Liza could have drawn one.

Still, I had to see what Dana was talking about. "Excuse me," I shouted as I forced my way through the wall of Pops to get a good look at Liza's exhibit.

I wasn't surprised at how amazing the paintings were. They were lifelike, but each had little touches that made them cute or funny – like the way Marc was holding his camera over one eye, or how Felicia and Rachel were twirling basketballs on their pointer fingers.

What was surprising, however, was the picture in the middle of the display. It was the smallest of all, but it had two people in it – Liza and me. Yes, me! We were in Liza's backyard. I was standing on my head, and Liza was standing upright next to me.

Liza came over as I was staring at the painting. "You remember that day?" she asked me. "We were trying to do yoga on my back lawn, and my dad came out and took that picture."

I smiled. "What I remember is when I stood up, my hair was covered in mud," I said. "I hadn't realized how wet the grass was."

Liza giggled. "It took you forever to wash the mud out of your hair."

"And then we had to wash the ring of mud out of your shower," I added with a laugh. "Good times."

"*Really* good times," Liza agreed. "That's why I had to put this painting in here. I used the photograph as my model for the sketch."

"But I only apologized to you yesterday," I reminded her. "When did you do this?"

"Wednesday afternoon," Liza said. "I told you, even though I didn't know why you were mad at me, I knew we'd make up eventually."

"So this is what you meant when you said I was part of the project," I said.

Liza smiled. "Exactly," she told me. "You were here more than just in spirit. After all you've done for me, I had to draw you in."

"I'm glad you did," I told her.

"I am, too," she agreed.

Dana let out a little groan. "Jenny, you are so corny," she said. Then she turned to Liza. "Which is why you need us around," she said. "We'll let you know whether something is corny or cool."

"I think she can figure that out all on her own," I said, defending my friend.

"Clearly that's not true," Sabrina countered. She glared at me.

Just then, my parents and Aunt Amy arrived in the front hall. They were standing behind us, looking at the series of portraits Liza had completed. My aunt walked over and wrapped her arm around Liza's shoulders.

"This is even more incredible than I'd imagined," she told her.

"Thank you," Liza said.

"And it's helped me decide that your greeting card should definitely have kids, not animals, on it," she added.

Maya gave Liza a smug look. "See?" she said. "We told you so."

Liza shrugged. "I guess you were right."

"In fact," my aunt continued, "you have the perfect drawing right here."

"I do?" Liza asked.

"She does?" Dana, Sabrina, Addie, Maya, and Claire echoed.

Aunt Amy nodded. "That one in the middle. The one where Jenny is on her head, and you're standing right next to her."

"Really?" I asked, surprised.

My aunt nodded. "Inside it can say something like, 'Thanks for being my friend through all the ups and downs.'"

Liza smiled. "That's perfect!" she exclaimed. "It's amazing how you just thought that up."

"Thanks," Aunt Amy said with a grin. She pulled out her camera phone and snapped a few pictures of the painting. "I'm going to send these to the New York office so they can be ready to print when you send them the art." She paused for a minute. "Do you remember the way I told you to ship the painting for safekeeping?"

Liza nodded. "I have it all written down. I'll take it home at the end of the art show, wrap it up, and bring it to the post office tomorrow."

"Terrific!" Aunt Amy said with a smile.

Suddenly I noticed that my friends and family had a much clearer view of Liza's art project. All of the Pops had moved away. They were no longer the least bit interested in Liza, the paintings, or the greeting cards. Once they realized none of them was going to be modeling for Liza's card, there was no reason for them to stick around.

Which was just fine with me, because it left more room in the hallway for Chloe and her parents. They had just arrived in the main hall of the school, along with Sam and her mom.

"Hey, Jenny," Chloe greeted me. "Isn't this amazing?"

"Totally," I agreed. I smiled at Liza. She smiled back at me. There were no hard feelings. That's the cool thing about my friends. Sometimes we have arguments or disagreements, but they never last very long.

"Blimey, Liza," Sam's mother said. "I had no idea you were such an amazing artist. I love the way you painted the Union Jack behind the drawing you did of my little Sam-monster!"

"Mum!" Sam shouted. She was clearly embarrassed by her mother's nickname for her. I could tell by the way she blushed and then turned to see if the Pops were still within earshot. Luckily, they didn't seem to have noticed anything my friends or their parents were saying. We were no longer of any interest to them.

"So, uh, what's with those two teachers?" Aunt Amy asked my friends and me. She was clearly trying to change the subject for Sam's sake. Sam smiled at her gratefully. Aunt Amy gave her a quick wink.

"Which two teachers?" Josh asked my aunt.

"The redhead in the corner, and that dark-haired guy near the front door," she answered.

I turned around and took a glance at the corner and the door. Not that I really had to look. I pretty much already knew that the redheaded teacher was Ms. Young, and the dark-haired guy was Mr. Strapp.

"What about them?" I asked my aunt.

"Are they married?"

"Not yet," Chloe told her. "But my guess is they'll be engaged any day now."

"That's my guess, too," Aunt Amy agreed.

"How can you tell?" I asked her.

"It's just something in the way they're looking at each other," she replied. "They haven't taken their eyes off of each other the entire time we've been standing here."

Chloe was beaming. "I'm so glad you said that," she told my aunt. "I've been trying to tell people they were dating, but none of my friends would listen."

"That's because it's not *your* place to tell people about them," Liza reminded Chloe.

Chloe laughed. "Well, somebody has to do it," she joked.

"How about we leave gossiping to the Pops?" I suggested to her. "They do it better than anyone."

"That's true," Felicia said. "And they don't even wait to find out if the rumors they're spreading are true."

"Which is why no one pays attention to them," Liza said.

"All right, you guys have convinced me," Chloe said. "I promise to keep my lips zipped about Ms. Young and Mr. Strapp. But that doesn't mean I'm going to stop keeping an eye on them."

"Me, either," Felicia agreed. "It's kind of like having our own romance movie playing right here at school. Aren't we lucky?"

I looked at my friends, who had all gathered to congratulate Liza on her success. The nicest thing about that was that it wasn't unusual. My friends and I do that sort of thing for one another all the time. It's great to know that if you're good at something, or if you just want to try something new, you have plenty of people to cheer you on. And if you make a mistake, those same people will still be there, helping you to feel better and move on.

I grinned at Felicia. "We *are* lucky," I agreed. "Definitely."

Which Movie Character Are You?

MOVIES ARE a lot like middle school. In almost every one there's a drama queen, a brooding artist, a brain, and a jock. Ever wonder what part you'd play? To find out what movie character you're most like, take this quickie quiz.

1. What's your favorite class in school?

    A. I really like English class.

    B. I can't wait for gym!

    C. Math's my fave.

    D. Whatever. It's all school to me.

2. What's in your backpack besides your books?

    A. My journal and my camera.

    B. A water bottle.

    C. My calculator and thesaurus.

    D. Lip gloss and eyeliner.

3. How would you describe your latest crush?

A. Mysterious.

B. Full of school spirit.

C. Serious.

D. Which of my crushes are you talking about? I have so many!

4. It's the day of your school's championship basketball game. Where can you be found?

A. At a foreign film festival at the local movie theater.

B. On the court!

C. Keeping score.

D. Cheerleading.

5. What's your idea of a dream vacation?

A. A trip to a quiet beach where I can lie on the sand, feel the sun on my body, and listen to the waves.

B. Hiking in the mountains.

C. Visiting European historical museums.

D. I'm going to Broadway, baby!

6. Where do you head first when you go to the mall?

A. I rarely go to the mall. I like vintage thrift shops better.

B. The sporting goods store.

C. Definitely the electronics store.

D. The makeup counter at the department store.

7. When you have a fight with your BFF, how do you handle it?

A. I hide in my room and write angry poetry.

B. I go for a long run to work out my fury.

C. I put it out of my head and focus on something else.

D. I hit the phones and tell everyone I know what happened!

8. It's time for a visit to the hairdresser. What style do you have in mind?

A. I'm thinking of getting purple highlights.

B. I don't care as long as I can tie it back in a ponytail.

C. I want some bangs. I hate it when my hair falls in my eyes while I'm trying to read.

D. I want a radical change. I think I'm going to go really short, or maybe even get a Mohawk!

So, based on your answers, what role would you get cast in for the next teen movie?

Mostly As: You are the **brooding artist**. You don't have time to get caught up in middle school drama. You're too busy thinking deep thoughts and writing poetry or creating gloomy paintings.

Mostly Bs: You're a total **jock**. As long as you're on the field, the ice, or the court, you're one happy girl.

Mostly Cs: You are definitely a **brainiac**. You're dedicated to good grades, and you're not going let anything stand in the way of those A's.

Mostly Ds: A **drama queen** like you can always be found at the center of the latest middle school dilemma. Whether you're involved in your own issues, or helping out a friend, somehow you always wind up in the middle of the mess. But that's okay, because that's where you are happiest.

Will Jenny survive middle school?
Read these books to find out!

#1 Can You Get an F in Lunch?
Jenny's best friend, Addie, dumps her
on the first day of middle school.

#2 Madame President
Jenny and Addie both run for
class president. Who will win?

#3 I Heard a Rumor
The school gossip columnist
is revealing everyone's secrets!

#4 The New Girl
There's a new girl in school!
Will she be a Pop or not?

#5 Cheat Sheet
Could one of Jenny's friends
be a cheater?

#6 P.S. I Really Like You
Jenny has a secret admirer!
Who could it be?

#7 Who's Got Spirit?
It's Spirit Week! Who has the most school pride — Jenny's friends or the Pops?

#8 It's All Downhill From Here

Jenny has to spend her snow day with her ex-BFF, Addie!

#9 Caught in the Web
Jenny and her friends start a webcast, and so do the Pops! Which show will have more viewers?

#10 Into the Woods

The sixth grade goes to science camp and Jenny, Sam, and Chloe have to share a cabin with the Pops!

#11 Wish Upon a Star
Can Jenny work with Addie to save the winter dance?

Super Special: How the Pops Stole Christmas

Everyone's in a holiday mood except the Pops. Will they ruin Christmas for Jenny?